THE ROYAL BALLET SCHOOL

Diaries

6

Grace's Show of Strength

THE ROYAL BALLET SCHOOL

Diaries

6

Grace's Show
of Strength

Written by Alexandra Moss

Grosset & Dunlap

For Tom Powell, with lots of love—A.M.

Special thanks to Sue Mongredie

GROSSET & DUNLAP
Published by the Penguin Group
Penguin Group (USA) Inc., 375 Hudson Street, New York, New York 10014, U.S.A.
Penguin Group (Canada), 90 Eglinton Avenue East, Suite 700, Toronto, Ontario, Canada M4P 2Y3
(a division of Pearson Penguin Canada Inc.)
Penguin Books Ltd, 80 Strand, London WC2R 0RL, England
Penguin Ireland, 25 St Stephen's Green, Dublin 2, Ireland
(a division of Penguin Books Ltd)
Penguin Group (Australia), 250 Camberwell Road, Camberwell, Victoria 3124, Australia
(a division of Pearson Australia Group Pty Ltd)
Penguin Books India Pvt Ltd, 11 Community Centre, Panchsheel Park, New Delhi - 110 017, India
Penguin Group (NZ), Cnr Airborne and Rosedale Roads, Albany, Auckland 1310, New Zealand
(a division of Pearson New Zealand Ltd)
Penguin Books (South Africa) (Pty) Ltd, 24 Sturdee Avenue, Rosebank, Johannesburg 2196, South Africa

Penguin Books Ltd, Registered Offices:
80 Strand, London WC2R 0RL, England

Series created by Working Partners Ltd.

Copyright © 2005 by Working Partners Ltd. All rights reserved. Published by Grosset & Dunlap, a division of Penguin Young Readers Group, 345 Hudson Street, New York, New York 10014. GROSSET & DUNLAP is a trademark of Penguin Group (USA) Inc. Printed in the U.S.A.

Library of Congress Cataloging-in-Publication Data

Moss, Alexandra.
  Grace's show of strength / written by Alexandra Moss.
    p. cm. — (The Royal Ballet School diaries ; #6)
  Summary: In the last weeks of their first year at the Royal Ballet School, as they face exams and extra rehearsals for an end-of-year performance at the Royal Opera House, Ellie becomes very concerned about Grace's odd behavior.
  ISBN 0-448-43772-4
  [1. Ballet dancing—Fiction. 2. Friendship—Fiction. 3. Obsessive-compulsive disorder—Fiction. 4. Boarding schools—Fiction. 5. Schools—Fiction. 6. Royal Ballet. School—Fiction. 7. London (England)—Fiction. 8. England—Fiction.] I. Title. II. Series.
  PZ7.M8515Gra 2006
  [Fic]—dc22   2005023074

10 9 8 7 6 5 4 3 2 1

Dear Diary,

I'm writing this curled up in bed. Tonight's my last night at home with Mom and Steve for a while. The summer half-term vacation here in Oxford has just flown by. This time tomorrow, I'll be back in my Royal Ballet School bed, whispering with all the other Year 7 girls after dorm lights-out!

I can't believe that we're already at the end of our first year at The Royal Ballet School. It seems like hardly any time at all since I arrived there last September—all nervous and excited, knowing almost no one. And yet, now I can't imagine being anywhere else. I feel like I've been a Royal Ballet School student forever.

I hope I can get to sleep tonight.

My mind is buzzing at the thought of tomorrow, and it's really hot tonight, too. Summer in England kind of takes you by surprise, I've decided. You get a little warm spell in late spring and think, *Hey, summer's here!* And then it suddenly turns chilly again. And after a while—when you begin thinking it's going to stay overcast and showery forever—a hot spell comes along and catches everyone off guard! Must remember to pack my sunglasses before I leave in the morning.

We've been told that the weeks ahead will be even more hectic than usual. We've got tons of end-of-year academic exams to plow through. (Bad!) But as well as studying like crazy, we'll be rehearsing our socks off for the School's end-of-year performances at The Royal Opera House. (Good!!!) I'm determined to dance absolutely perfectly. The most exciting thing ever will be taking part in the grand finale on The Royal Opera House main stage—alongside the WHOLE SCHOOL! WOW!!

That part of the show is called the *Grand Défilé* and Jessica, my Year 8 guide, told me that dancing in it last summer was just the most exciting thing she'd ever, ever done. I know already that I'm going to feel the same way. It's going to be AWESOME!

Ellie Brown pushed open the door to the long, crescent-shaped dormitory where the twelve Year 7 girls slept, a big smile on her face. It was always really exciting to see her friends again and to catch up on everybody's news. Even when they'd been away from school for just a week, like now, there always seemed to be tons to talk about. Somehow living with her schoolmates and seeing them every single day of school, for breakfast, lunch, and dinner, for ballet, biology, and bedtime, made their friendships even stronger. Being away from one another only made Ellie realize just how close they all were. Boy, had she missed them!

"Hi, guys!" she called, stepping into the dorm. She was fully expecting to be mobbed by her best friends—Grace, Sophie, Lara, Kate, Isabelle, and Bryony—as she usually was. But silence greeted her words.

Ellie looked up and down the empty dorm, feeling puzzled. Could she really be the first person to arrive back at school today? She knew that Lara, coming from Ireland, could be stuck at the airport. Perhaps Sophie, who lived in the northern city of Manchester, had been caught in heavy traffic in her long journey down to school. But where were the others? Grace only lived an hour or so away, as did Isabelle. And though she could imagine Isabelle being delayed by one of her arguments with her mom, perfectionist Grace was never late for anything, ever.

Ellie's shoulders slumped a little as she heaved her bags over to her bed. She'd been so excited to see everyone that she'd said her good-byes to her mom down in the car park outside school, just so she could rush up to the dorm as soon as possible. Now that she was here without anyone to talk to, being back at school almost felt like an anticlimax.

Then Ellie noticed a couple of the dorm windows were open. And actually, now that she came to think of it, the place wasn't looking half as neat as it had at the end of last term . . . The smile returned to her face as she realized there were suitcases and bags by all of her friends' beds. And there, on her own bed, was a scrawled note:

> Ellie! We're outside, around the back.
> Come and find us as soon as you arrive!
> Love,
> The girls
> xxxxx

Ellie's smile broadened. She snatched up her sunglasses. Unpacking could wait. Now . . . where were her friends?

Hurrying out of the dorm, Ellie rushed across the airy

reception area and through the Salon. Its two huge French windows led out onto a stone balcony, with steps leading down to the School's gardens. Outside, the sun was blazing down through the tall trees that edged the grounds of White Lodge, the magnificent historic house that was home to The Royal Ballet Lower School.

Hundreds of years ago, the building had actually been a royal hunting lodge. Even now, in the twenty-first century, Ellie found it easy to imagine noblemen galloping through the leafy parkland that surrounded White Lodge, and lords and ladies swishing grandly around the grounds. Her friends back home in Chicago certainly got a kick out of it when she'd e-mailed them to say that she had some of her academic classes in what had once been the king of England's stable block!

Ellie leaned on the warm, lichen-speckled stone balustrade as she scanned the lawn in front of her. No lords or ladies to be seen today; instead, clusters of Royal Ballet School students— some sitting in the shade of the huge cedar trees, others stretched out to tan on the grass, their arms and legs glistening with sunscreen. Some of the older boys were messing around with a soccer ball—*football*, Ellie corrected herself with a smile— practicing penalty shots by the looks of things, while a group of girls had set up a game of badminton. But no sign of Sophie and the others so far . . .

"Ellie! Hey, Ellie! Over here!"

Aha! A girl with braids snaking out from under her sun hat was standing up and waving madly at her from a spot on the lawn, way over to Ellie's left. Grace! And the others were with her, too! Ellie waved back and then hurried down the stone steps and over the grass toward them.

Sophie was leaning up on her elbows and grinning at Ellie, her silver aviator shades gleaming in the sunlight. Lara was pushing her red ponytail out of the way under her green and white "Ireland" baseball cap. And there was Isabelle, her nose white with sunblock, wearing huge Jackie O. sunglasses!

"You guys look as if you're in disguise," Ellie giggled, slipping her own sunglasses down onto her nose as she reached them. "No wonder I couldn't spot you right away."

"We thought we'd set you a challenge," Sophie joked, jumping up and hugging her warmly. "Test your powers of observation."

"Well, if you decide to abandon the stage for the FBI, you'll make a great undercover agent," Ellie laughed. She spoke the words lightly, but felt a little sad: This was to be Sophie's last half-term at The Royal Ballet School. Unfortunately, she'd been "assessed out" of the Lower School. They'd all been desperately sad about it. But Sophie had received lots of support and advice from The Royal Ballet School about what to do instead. She had applied for, and been given, a place at a performing arts school in her home city of Manchester, which was much more suitable for her musical theater talent and that wonderful voice of hers. She was really eager to start there in September. Ellie wished her all the luck in the world—but knew she was going to badly miss her vivacious friend.

"So, how is everybody?" Ellie asked, settling herself comfortably down on the grass, once she'd hugged the others in turn. "And does anyone know when Kate and Bryony are due back?"

"I think Kate's going to be in late tonight," Lara said, picking a couple of daisies from the lawn and splitting their stems with a thumbnail to make a daisy chain. "You know it's her birthday today? Well, she texted me to say that she's having a day of treats with her parents out in the West End. Sounds good to me."

"Definitely," Ellie said, feeling pleased for her friend. Kate had had a tough few weeks earlier in the term. "And Bryony?"

"Due back any minute," Sophie replied. "We left a note on her bed, too."

"Great," Ellie sighed, feeling contented. "I can't wait to have us all back together again. I missed you all so much. Crazy, isn't it? Just a week—but it felt like forever!"

"I know," Isabelle said from behind her thick, dark glasses. "It felt like a long week to me, too. My mother has a new boyfriend and . . ." She shrugged, and Ellie could imagine her rolling her eyes melodramatically behind her dark lenses. "How do you say? I am not chuffing about it."

Sophie spluttered with laughter. "*Chuffed*, Isabelle. You'd say that you weren't *chuffed* about it."

The others giggled, too. Isabelle was French, and her English was generally excellent—although she sometimes struggled with the slang phrases the English girls used. Ellie knew how she felt. When she'd started school in England for the first time, she'd been amazed to discover just what a different language American English was from British English!

"Why don't you like him?" Grace asked curiously, propping herself up on one elbow and brushing a few stray grass seeds off her T-shirt.

Isabelle spread her hands expressively. "He is okay, I think. A little . . . *ordinary*, perhaps, but that is not so bad, I suppose. No, *he* is not the problem," she said. "I think that, in my heart, I was hoping my father would come and make things up with my mother. Yet here she is with somebody else." She sighed, and shrugged again. "So my dreams of a happy family are over."

There was a pause. "Well . . ." Ellie started, trying to think of the right words of sympathy to say.

"And he is *bald*, too," Isabelle suddenly snorted. "Bald—and with a beard. I mean . . . It is not good, is it? I have told her—bald is not good, but will she listen to me, her daughter? *Non*. And I have to walk down the street with this man!"

Everyone laughed, and the seriousness of the moment passed.

"Isabelle, give him a break!" Lara said. "My dad's going a little bald, and he's all right." She paused. "Okay, so he's not like a pinup or anything—he wouldn't win any awards for his looks—but it doesn't stop me from walking down the street with him!"

Sophie placed a circlet of daisies on top of Isabelle's head. "I pronounce you Princess of the Hairbrush," she said. "Beware any hairless ones who step into your path!"

Isabelle started to laugh, too, as she bowed her head regally. "It is true," she confessed. "I am cruel and unforgiving." She sipped her drink. "But you love me for it, *non?*"

"Hello, everyone!" came a sweet voice just then.

Ellie looked up to see Bryony running the last few steps over the grass to them, and jumped up, happy to see her again. "Hey, Bryony." She smiled, hugging her. "Did you have a good vacation?"

Bryony sat down and began smearing herself with sunscreen. "Yes," she said. "But I'm so excited to be back again—especially with the end-of-year performances to look forward to!"

"Ooh, yes," Sophie agreed at once, stretching one bare leg in the air and grabbing hold of her toes. "Curtain call for Ms. Crawford! Your fans are calling for you!" she said in a high nasal voice. She grinned. "Well, maybe I'll hear it one day."

"I can't wait for the *Grand Défilé*," said Lara. "Won't that be something? The whole school onstage together!" She looked shivery with excitement at the thought.

"Me neither," Ellie agreed. "It's going to be awesome. Can you imagine, looking around, seeing everyone you know from school there onstage with you? What a thrill!"

"It will be wonderful," Isabelle added with a smile. "The perfect way to mark the end of our time as Year 7 girls, I think."

"Oh, don't . . ." Bryony begged, her eyes looking a little misty. "I can't bear to think of Year 7 ending." She shot a look at Sophie, and Ellie guessed what she was thinking: No more Year 7 meant no more Sophie at The Royal Ballet School.

Sophie smiled at Bryony and gave her an affectionate nudge. "Hey, guys!" she said brightly. "I've just thought: You'll be Year 8 guides to the new Year 7 students. Can you imagine?"

Ellie hadn't thought about that either, until now! On joining The Royal Ballet School, each new student was assigned a "family" to offer them support during their time at the school. Ellie's own Year 8 guide was Jessica Walters. Ellie often talked to her if she needed advice. It was strange to think that she'd soon take on that role herself for a younger student. "Wow," she said. "I remember being in awe of the Year 8s. It's weird, thinking that the next Year 7s will think that way about us."

"Once we've been on the main stage of The Royal Opera House for the *Grand Défilé*, dah-ling, they'll be even more in awe of us," joked Lara. "Hey, we'll have to ask Megan about it—her sister's in Year 9, isn't she?"

"Yes, that's right," Ellie said. Megan was another of the Year 7 girls. She slept on the other side of the dorm from Ellie's group of friends.

"Well, I'm sure I heard Megan say that she'd been to last year's performance, to watch her sister dance," Lara went on. "And this year she and her sister will be on the same stage together . . ."

From the faraway look in her eyes, Ellie guessed that Lara was thinking about her own sister back in Ireland. Lara came from a very close-knit family and Ellie knew how hard she'd found it at first, coming to boarding school and being away from home.

Just then, a call came up from one of the housemothers who'd appeared on the balcony. "Dinnertime! Come in and wash your hands!"

Everybody got to their feet, gathered up their things, and began to head off to the canteen, still animatedly discussing the end-of-year performances.

Ellie noticed Grace was hanging behind a little. "Come on, slowpoke," she called out jokily. "We'll be last in line for dinner!"

Grace was brushing grass off herself. "Have I got grass stains on these shorts?" she groaned aloud. "Mum will kill me if I have— these are brand-new."

"You're fine," Ellie assured her. "Come on, let's catch up with the others—I don't want to miss any of the conversation, do you?"

"No, 'course not . . ." Grace mumbled.

Ellie caught the subdued note in Grace's voice. She remembered how stressed her friend always got at the prospect of dancing in public. At least there wouldn't be any auditions for the end-of-year performances. Grace tended to go to pieces in such high-pressure situations.

Ellie slipped an arm through Grace's. "So, what did you get up to last week?" she said, changing the subject deliberately. She'd find out what else had been said about the end-of-year performances later, she thought.

Grace seemed to cheer up a little as she told Ellie about the new video camera her mom had bought, and how she and her friends had been making home movies together. "It was such fun," she said, a smile breaking out over her face. "Next time I'm home, I'll copy some onto a videocassette and bring it to school so you can watch."

"Great," Ellie said, as they walked back into school together. The smell of food from the canteen hit her and she realized just how hungry she was. How could it be that just talking with her friends gave her such an appetite? She smiled as she joined the line and saw some of the other girls from her year, Holly and Alice, oh and there was Megan, too . . . . Oh, it was good to be back. How she loved being at The Royal Ballet School!

Dear Diary,
     Here I am, back in my school bed for the last stretch of Year 7 time. It's weird to think that these are my last few weeks of

being together with all eleven of my dorm-
sisters. In Year 8, we get split into groups
to share smaller dorms.

This evening, after dinner, we piled
into the common room we share with the
Year 8 girls to watch a movie on TV.
But during the first commercial we began
discussing the end-of-year performances
again, and the movie was forgotten.

Jessica and some of the other Year 8
girls were telling us about what it was like
dancing in last year's performances. They're
really excited about this year's, too.

The only person who doesn't seem to be
excited yet is Grace. She's such a fantastic
dancer, but her nerves always seem to get
the better of her. I just know she's probably
dreading the prospect of dancing at The
Royal Opera House. It's SUCH a shame!

Anyway, as we were all talking, Grace
got up, saying that she wanted to get in
some ballet practice so that she wouldn't
feel too rusty in tomorrow's class. I kind of
knew what she meant—just a week away from
regular classes always makes me feel a little

slow. I was half-thinking of joining her, just
to keep her company. But then Kate arrived,
with an enormous birthday cake covered in
whipped cream and strawberries. And that
kind of made my mind up for me!

Kate looked really happy. For every other
vacation she's gone to stay in Newcastle with
her grandmother, because her parents were
working abroad. But this time, her parents
were in London, so she stayed the whole week
with them. They had a great time, by the
sound of it.

The cake didn't last long—the common
room was so full that between us all, we
managed to polish off the whole thing while
we were catching up. Bliss!!

chapter 2

There was a great buzz of excitement in the air as Ellie and her friends limbered up before their Monday ballet class the following morning. There was always something nice about returning to daily class after being away, Ellie thought, as she stretched out her left leg on the barre. But this morning, there was the added thrill of anticipation: Ms. Wells, their teacher, was bound to mention the end-of-year performances!

Ellie leaned over her leg, feeling the stretch and pull of her hamstring as the muscle warmed up. She flexed her foot, and then pointed her toes. Flex, point, flex, point. *What will the Year 7s be asked to dance?* she wondered. *And how exactly does the* Grand Défilé *work?*

She was just about to lean across to Grace, who was next to her at the barre, and ask her what she thought, when the door opened. Ms. Wells came in, followed by the pianist who accompanied their classes.

"Hello, everyone," their teacher said warmly as she smiled around the room at them all. "Lovely to see you looking so fit and healthy! Did everybody have a nice half-term break?"

"Yes, Ms. Wells," the girls all chorused. There was an expectant silence, each of them keeping her eyes on Ms. Wells. It was as if they were all willing her to start talking about the end-of-year performances, Ellie thought.

Ms. Wells looked a little startled to have twelve pairs of eyes fixed so steadfastly upon her. Then she chuckled. "Something tells me you're waiting for me to make some kind of announcement— about the end-of-year performances, perhaps?" Her eyes twinkled.

"Yes!" Sophie blurted out, abandoning her warm-up at once.

"We're just wondering when we'll find out what we'll be doing," Ellie said eagerly.

"And when will the rehearsals begin?" added Kate.

"And does *everybody* have to take part?" Grace asked in a quiet voice.

Ellie shot her a sympathetic look, but nobody else seemed to have heard her.

"All right!" Ms. Wells laughed, holding up her hands as if to try to stop the flood of questions. "I'd better start giving you some answers, then."

The studio fell silent. Ellie couldn't wait to hear more.

"The end-of-year performances will be taking place, as usual, during the first half of July," Ms. Wells began. "As I'm sure you all know, the performances take place in the Linbury Studio Theater at The Royal Opera House—except for the final Saturday matinee— which is performed on The Royal Opera House main stage, and is completed with the *Grand Défilé*."

Lara gave Ellie an excited nudge.

"The Linbury performance programs vary," Ms. Wells continued. "Some feature both Upper School and Lower School students—some just Lower School. This year, the Friday evening program features just Lower School—and is when you and the Year 7 boys will be performing."

This time, Ellie gave Lara an excited nudge.

"We've decided that the Year 7 contribution to the Linbury program this year will be a character dancing piece," Ms. Wells continued. "You have character class with Ms. O'Connor this afternoon, don't you?" she asked. Everyone nodded. "Well, Ms. O'Connor will tell you more about the piece she's chosen for you then," Ms. Wells told them. "And I'll be joining forces with Mr. Shah, the Year 7 boys' teacher, to work with you all on Year 7's contribution to the *Grand Défilé*."

"What exactly happens in the *Grand Défilé*, Ms. Wells?" Lara asked excitedly.

Ms. Wells smiled. "The best way I can describe the *Grand Défilé* is that it builds and builds, rather like a symphony in music," she began. "First, the Year 7 students come onstage to dance a short piece. And then, as they leave, the Year 8 students arrive onstage to take their turn. And as the Year 8s leave, the Year 9s arrive—and so on, up through every year of the school. As the students get older, their pieces become more and more complex—until the graduates come onstage to dance the final, most impressive piece. And then . . ." Ms. Wells paused. "The whole school runs back onstage together to line up in perfectly straight year rows and take a final bow before the curtain comes down."

"Wow!" breathed Sophie, unable to keep silent any longer. "It sounds sooo wonderful!"

"It is," Megan said, her eyes shining. "Just wait—it's amazing."

Ms. Wells nodded. "Seeing the whole school onstage together like that always sends a shiver down my spine," she agreed. "Now . . ." she went on, "you might think that your three-minute performance for the *Grand Défilé* doesn't sound very much to prepare for. But you will all have to be *absolutely perfect* during those three minutes. *Everyone* will be watching you! So preparation starts on Wednesday: First rehearsal is at five p.m., and Mr. Shah and I will begin working on the piece with you then."

A gasp of surprise went around the room. Ellie stared at Ms. Wells, wondering if she'd heard her correctly.

"Wednesday, as in *this* Wednesday?" Sophie asked. "As in two days' time?"

Ms. Wells nodded. "That's right," she told them. "Mr. Shah and I have already started putting together choreography ideas. And on Wednesday we'll start by pairing you all into girl-boy partners." She gave them a winning smile. "It's going to be another busy term for you girls—but just think about the end result!"

Ellie didn't know whether to feel more flustered or excited as she and the other girls finished warming up for their class. "It's all happening so quickly, isn't it?" she whispered.

In front of her, Grace replied with a tense little nod.

"Fine with me," said Lara, who was on the other side of Ellie. "I can't wait for it all to start," she said happily, sinking into a perfect *plié*. "I just can't wait!"

•   •   •   •

After ballet class was over, Ellie and her friends rushed upstairs to shower and change as usual, before their academic classes started. Of course, there was only one topic of conversation.

"Doesn't it all sound wonderful?" Bryony said happily as they all hurried to the dormitory. "The *Grand Défilé* sounds absolutely amazing."

"I can't wait for character class this afternoon," Sophie agreed, grinning. "I wonder what Ms. O'Connor's got lined up for us? And our first rehearsal for the *Grand Défilé* is on Wednesday!"

"I am glad, I think, that it is happening quickly," said Isabelle, pulling her gleaming brown hair out from its bun and shaking it down over her shoulders. "We will not have time to get worried."

"Speak for yourself," Grace muttered. She pushed open the dorm door, which seemed to make a sigh. "I'm worried already!"

"Oh, Grace," Ellie said, trying to sound comforting. "You always say that—but it's never as bad as you think."

"No, it's usually worse," Grace replied, stripping off her ballet clothes by her bed and grabbing her shower things.

Shaking her head, Ellie picked up her own toiletries and followed her friend to the bathroom.

How awful to feel like that about something that should be so fun, Ellie thought as she turned on one of the showers and stepped beneath the hot cascade of water. Her own feelings were mainly of excitement, not dread. Sure, she knew that she'd get a brief jolt of nerves right before she had to dance onstage—but in some ways, that adrenaline rush drove her on to dance her best when she knew it really mattered. Whereas with Grace, although she was technically one of the best dancers in their year, she could never seem to let her ability shine through and *enjoy* her dancing while she was performing. Her nerves always seemed to get in the way.

Ellie finished her shower and saw that Grace had already made her way back to the dorm. The conversation in there was still all about the summer performances.

"I wonder who will get the best parts," Sophie mused aloud, as she buttoned up her blouse.

Grace, who was nearest to Sophie, didn't reply—but Lara had no such hesitation in continuing the conversation. "I must call home to see if the family has organized flights over here from Ireland yet," she said chattily as she fastened her skirt. "They're planning to arrive on Friday for our Linbury performance, and then they're going to tour around England for a week until the final Saturday matinee."

"I'm just dying to find out what character dance we'll be doing," Bryony said excitedly.

Kate nodded. "Me too," she said. "I wish we could see into the future so that we didn't have to wait to find out."

Ellie chuckled. "There's only one person around here who can see into the future," she said in a low, spooky kind of voice. "And she is, of course . . ."

"Madame Sophie!" the other girls chorused.

Ellie grinned across at Sophie, who was very into astrology and tarot cards.

"Funny you should say that," Sophie said, digging around in her cupboard, "because I've been meaning to try out my new fortune-telling game ever since we got back to school."

"Oh, no, don't encourage her, you lot!" Grace exclaimed. She had no patience for Sophie's so-called psychic powers. "We haven't got time, Soph. Math starts in ten minutes."

"You can find out a lot in ten minutes," Sophie replied loftily. She then pulled out a flat, purple cardboard box and brandished it in the air. "Ta-da!" she cried. "The answers to all of your questions can be found in this box, girls. Who wants to try it out with me? All you have to do is ask . . ."

"Go on, then," Lara said. "I'll go first. I'd like to ask the mystic cardboard box: Will I get picked for a good part in our end-of-year performance?"

Sophie took a pack of cards from the box and started shuffling with great ceremony.

"Eight minutes to go," Grace said, hurriedly pulling on her shoes.

"Lara McCloud, you asked the cards if you'd be chosen for a good part in the end-of-year performance . . ." Sophie said in a mysterious-sounding voice. "And the cards predict . . . Oh." She'd turned over a card that had an enormous purple question mark on it. "*'The spirits are unclear,'*" she read aloud. "So what that means is . . ."

". . . You don't know," Lara replied, with a laugh. "So much for the cards providing me with an answer!"

"Well, it's still an *answer*," Sophie argued, "even if the answer is 'Nobody knows.' "

"Hmm . . ." Lara said, gathering together her math books. "Not so sure about this game, Soph. I think I prefer your crystal ball."

Sophie slumped her shoulders dejectedly.

"I'll ask one," Ellie said gamely, intrigued despite Lara's inconclusive answer. "Same question for me, please, cards: Will I get picked for a good part in the show?"

Sophie perked up and shuffled up the cards again. Then she repeated the question and turned one over. The picture on it was of a man with a black cloud above his head. "Um . . . *'No man can stop the rain,'*" Sophie read aloud. "Which means . . . er . . ."

Ellie laughed and turned her head toward the window, where she could see the sun blazing down outside. "Which means, I think you've bought a dud, Soph. Those cards are awful!"

Sophie opened her mouth as if she were about to protest, then laughed good-naturedly instead. "D'you know what, I think you're right," she said. "Maybe I'll stick to my horoscopes instead." She put the cards back into their purple box and sighed. "Off to math we go, then," she said. "And still none the wiser!"

Ellie picked up her math books and waited for Grace, who was now fixing her hair.

"I can't do a thing with it," Grace grumbled, brushing it hard.

Ellie watched as Grace made a face at her reflection, heaved a huge sigh, and then threw down her brush onto her bed. She was a little surprised. Her friend had always liked to be neat and tidy, yes—but she didn't usually do the prima donna thing. "Want me to give it a try?" Ellie offered.

"Yes, please," Grace replied. "I'm all thumbs today. I just can't get it right."

Ellie quickly fixed her friend's hair into a braid and fastened it with a band. "There," she said. "Will that do?"

"Thanks, Ellie," Grace replied gratefully, tucking in a few loose strands with a hair clip. "Are you sure I look okay?"

Ellie laughed. "Hey! What are you trying to say about my hairstyling skills?" she said playfully. "Of course you look okay. And it's only math class—you don't have to look like a glamour-puss for that!" She grabbed Grace's hand and pulled her along. "Come on, we'd better go before we're late."

Grace was unusually quiet as they walked to the math room together. Ellie broke the silence. "So, how are you feeling about the end-of-year performances?" she asked.

Grace didn't answer for a while. Then, with a funny little twist of her mouth, she turned to Ellie and said, "Well, let's put it this way: I'm not as excited about them as my mum is. She's already planning to film me dancing at The Royal Opera House with her new camcorder." Grace rolled her eyes, and then gave a shaky laugh. "That's the only reason she bought it, you know. She said as much when we were in the shop, choosing it." Grace hesitated for a moment, and then went on. "She was so disappointed when I didn't get chosen to dance in the *Nutcracker* production at The Royal Opera House last Christmas—but she knows that in the end-of-year performances, every student gets to go onstage. And she wants to capture the moment that I finally get to dance there."

Ellie shot her a look. Grace was smiling as she said all this, but her smile looked kind of forced. Ellie remembered how eager Grace's mom had been to find out where Grace ranked in their appraisals last term. She'd even called up the school to try to find out if Grace had been top of their year. Talk about pressure!

Ellie squeezed her friend's hand. "Just forget all that," she pleaded. "Just try to enjoy the ballet. You're such a great dancer— don't let the pressure spoil it for you again."

Grace gave Ellie a little nod. But she wouldn't meet her gaze.

Chapter

3

Ellie usually enjoyed her Monday afternoon classes. First was math, taught by Mr. Best. Then came drama, which was always fun, followed by English, which Ellie loved. Today, however, she was finding it hard to concentrate on anything her teachers said. All she could think about was how long it was until her character dancing class at the end of the afternoon. Just what did Ms. O'Connor have in store for them?

The end-of-class bell finally rang. "Class dismissed," Ms. Swaisland, their English teacher, said with an exasperated note in her voice. "And for your next class with me, please try to think more about English and a little less about ballet." She sighed and then gave the class a sympathetic smile. "I know you're all excited about the end-of-year performances," she continued, "but you have your end-of-year academic exams to think about, too. So make sure you concentrate when you do your English prep! Okay, guys?"

"Okay, Ms. Swaisland," Ellie and the others replied sheepishly.

But as soon as she left the classroom, Ellie's mind switched straight back to thinking about dancing again!

After English came tuck at four o'clock, when all of the

students could have a snack from their tuck boxes and a drink in the canteen. And then—at last!—it was time for character class.

Ellie and the others raced back to the dorm to change into their character clothes. Over their Year 7 pink leotards, they wore full circular black skirts with colorful stripes near the hem, and black leather character shoes with short white socks. The girls' character shoes were like Mary Jane shoes, with a black strap across the foot, a rounded toe, and a small heel. The Year 7 boys wore their normal ballet uniform of white short-sleeved leotard, blue lycra shorts, and short white socks—just adding their black character shoes.

When they were ready, the girls excitedly made their way down to their character class studio. Most of the boys were already there.

"Hey, Ellie!" called a friendly voice as she began warming up inside the studio.

Ellie smiled over at Matt Haslum as he came over to warm up next to her at the barre. "Hey, yourself," she replied. "So, do you think Ms. O'Connor will keep us as partners for the Year 7 Linbury performance?"

"Hope so," Matt answered with a smile. "We're like a pair of comfortable old shoes together now, aren't we?"

Ellie laughed and nodded. "Know what you mean," she said. She and Matt were old buddies. They'd first met before either of them had started Lower School, back when they'd been Junior

Associates of The Royal Ballet School, or JAs, as they were known. They, and Grace, had attended Saturday morning classes at the Upper School building in London's Covent Garden, and Ellie had partnered with Matt for the character dancing section of the class. When Matt had moved away to Birmingham, a city in central England, Ellie had missed him—so it had been a real joy to discover that Matt had been selected for Lower School, too, and they could once again be dancing partners.

Ms. O'Connor entered the studio with a clipboard tucked under one arm. She was striking to look at, with her flame-red hair and pale skin scattered with golden freckles. "Good afternoon, everyone," she said, in her lilting Scottish accent. "How are you all today?"

"Fine, thanks, Ms. O'Connor—but are you going to tell us what we're going to do for our Linbury performance today?" Matt burst out.

Ms. O'Connor laughed. "And hello to you, too, Matt!" she said, putting her clipboard down on top of the piano. "Yes, I did have a nice half-term break, thank you very much!" There was a pause, and then she put her hands on her hips, pretending to be exasperated. "Very well, I shall put you all out of your misery: Of *course* I'm going to tell you about your Linbury performance today—we're going to need to start work on it right away!"

Ellie felt a goose-bumpy sensation spread through her, and everybody started nudging one another in excitement.

"Let me tell you about the program that you will be part of, first of all," Ms. O'Connor said with a smile. "This year, you Year 7s will take part in the Friday evening performance—which is dedicated entirely to Lower School students. Some of the older students will perform ballet pieces specially choreographed for them. Others will perform pieces based on some of our national dances."

Lara nudged Ellie. "I can't wait until Year 8, when we start Irish dancing classes," she whispered. "I've already done loads of it back home."

"And you Year 7s will perform a character dance," Ms. O'Connor went on. "I've chosen something in the Polish Court style for you, featuring a step called the Holubetz. You'll stay with your usual partners, so you don't need to worry about getting used to a new partner's style just yet."

Ellie turned to smile at Matt, who gave her the thumbs-up sign.

"So, without further ado," Ms. O'Connor went on, "if you've all warmed up thoroughly, let's make a start by practicing the Holubetz steps. Partners, please!"

There was a buzz of excitement around the studio as the girls and boys partnered up.

"We'll practice the steps alone first, partners traveling toward and away from each other," Ms. O'Connor instructed. "And then we'll try them with partners together, turning in a circle while you hold on to each other around the waist."

She demonstrated the sequence of steps. "First position to start with, and then step across your body on your left foot—keeping the leg turned out, like so. Lower your head and eyes a little and lift your left arm to create an open, upward line, arm turning out at the elbow, palm facing down."

The class all copied her carefully.

"Now," Ms. O'Connor continued, "release your right leg to the side. Keep it low, Sophie, that's it! And then spring into the air—like this!" she said, deftly showing them the move. "The left leg needs to draw up to the right to click your heels in a *cabriole*. On the click, lift your head and eyes sharply, while rolling your lower arm inwards from the elbow, creating a curve with the palm up. Let's try that together."

Ellie repeated the movements with the rest of the class. It was more difficult than it looked. The click and the head movement were both precise, sharp movements, while the arm movement had to be soft and "oily," as Ms. O'Connor put it.

Then Ms. O'Connor showed them how to land on the left leg, release the right and deepen into a *fondu*, stepping out onto the right leg. "Then step across your body as before, ready to *cabriole* once more," she finished. "Let's try the whole thing together with partners a few times."

As Ellie and Matt faced each other and practiced the steps, all Ellie could think about was the fact that in just a few weeks, she and Matt would be dancing this sequence on the Linbury stage at The Royal Opera House. It was almost unbearably exciting and wonderful!

"Ellie, stop grinning at me like such a loon," Matt complained, with a laugh. "You're distracting me—I'm sure the ladies of the Polish Court never looked so manic!"

Ellie giggled. "Sorry, Matt," she said. "I'm just"—she clicked her heels as she jumped up, unable to wipe the beam off her face—"bouncing with happiness!"

•   •   •   •

At Wednesday afternoon's tuck, Ellie was surprised to find that she'd eaten a whole cereal bar while running through the Polish Holubetz steps in her head. "Did I actually just eat that?" she asked Grace in amazement, staring at the empty wrapper in front of her. "I don't remember putting a single bite of it into my mouth."

Grace didn't reply.

Ellie looked at her. Grace seemed tired—and had been a bit quiet all day, Ellie now realized. "You okay?" she asked.

Grace pushed away her half-eaten apple. "Ellie, I've been trying to tell you about the bad dream I had last night," she said.

"Oops—sorry, Grace. I was Polish dancing in my head!" Ellie explained sheepishly. "Tell me now," she invited.

"Never mind," said Grace. She sighed and stood up to throw her apple into the bin. "I suppose we'd better go and get ready for the first *Grand Défilé* rehearsal. We don't want to be late."

Ellie nodded. She and the rest of the girls followed suit, and then they all made their way back to the dorm to change.

Ellie couldn't stop humming cheerfully to herself as she pulled on her ballet uniform and coiled her hair neatly up into a bun. "Do you think we'll start learning the actual steps today?" she wondered aloud.

"We'll soon find out," Grace said through gritted teeth. She unfastened her bun for what must have been the third time and shook her hair over her shoulders. "Oh, my hair!" she cried, frowning at her reflection in the mirror. "I just can't get it right at the moment." She began brushing it fiercely. "Talk about a bad hair day—I think I'm having a bad hair *week*," she grumbled.

"Grace, your hair looks fine to me," Lara called out, raising her eyebrows at Ellie. Ellie raised her own eyebrows back at Lara, while Grace wasn't looking. Grace really was getting very finicky about her appearance these days, Ellie thought—and clearly, she wasn't the only person in the dorm to have noticed.

Grace began coiling up her hair in a bun once more. "Well, it doesn't look anything like fine to me," she replied. "It's official: My hair is a complete disaster zone!" She began thrusting bobby pins into her bun to hold it in place.

Ellie shook her head. "Grace Tennant, you're going to hurt yourself if you keep jabbing at your head like that," she said, going over and taking them out of her friend's hand. "Here—let me," she volunteered, putting in the last few bobby pins. "There. And it isn't a disaster zone. The only disaster will be if it takes us any longer to get ready for our first rehearsal!"

●　　　●　　　●　　　●

It was very strange, walking into the ballet studio with all the boys in their year, Ellie thought a few minutes later. Although they were in almost every other class together, ballet was something the girls and boys had always learned separately, so far. It was going to be interesting to have a rehearsal with Mr. Shah, the boys' teacher, too. She'd heard Matt and the other boys talk about him a lot, but hadn't had much to do with him herself before.

Ellie and Grace warmed up at the barre near Matt and a couple of the other boys, Justin and Toby. Excited whispers were passing from one person to the next as all the students speculated about what they would be asked to do.

After a few minutes, Ms. Wells and Mr. Shah came into the studio together. The whispers stopped abruptly and Ellie felt the hairs prickle up on the back of her neck. This was it! Their first *Grand Défilé* rehearsal was about to begin!

Ms. Wells spoke first. "Good afternoon, everyone," she said. "Today Mr. Shah and I are going to tell you about your *Grand Défilé* performance, and how we are going to prepare you for it."

Mr. Shah cleared his throat and took up the explanation. "First we shall divide you all into boy-girl couples of matching height—the smallest boy with the smallest girl, and so on," he began. "In our *Grand Défilé* piece, the smallest boy will lead all the boys onstage from the right—and the smallest girl will lead on all the girls from the left. The two groups will come together to form couples and perform a few steps, and then, all but two of the couples will separate again to line up on either side of the stage standing in *dégagé* pose: boys on one side, girls on the other; smallest in front, tallest at the back."

"The two couples remaining at center stage will then perform a short routine," Ms. Wells added.

Ellie's eyes widened with excitement. She looked over at Matt, who waggled his eyebrows up and down at her in reply. Ellie almost giggled.

"And then finally," Mr. Shah concluded, "the couples will come together again to run offstage and make way for the Year 8s."

"Remembering to quickly clear the wings, so as not to obstruct the Year 8s' access to the stage," Ms. Wells put in. "And then you must wait very quietly backstage," she said, "until it's time to run back onstage again with all the other year groups to form your military-precise rows for the final bow!"

She looked around at the group. "In case you were wondering, Mr. Shah and I shall choose the two central couples as rehearsals progress," she explained. "But for now, we're going to get the ball rolling by partnering you all up by height."

Ellie could feel her toes tingling already, longing to get started.

Sophie put up a hand. "What kind of thing will the central couples be doing?" she wanted to know.

"The girls will be doing *changements*," Ms. Wells replied.

"And the boys will be behind them, holding their waists," Mr. Shah added.

"Now, then," Ms. Wells went on, as a bout of whispering broke out among the students, "as I said, first we're going to work out the smallest to tallest boys and girls, and then have a play around with matching up couples. So girls, if you could line up, I can start putting you in order of height."

Ellie lined up with the girls at once and Ms. Wells stood back, sizing them up critically. "Bryony, you're probably the smallest," she said thoughtfully. "Then Kate . . . Then Alice . . . Then you, Ellie . . . or is Megan a little taller than you? Let's see . . . Hmmm, you're exactly the same. We'll have Ellie fourth and Megan fifth, I think, though . . ."

Mr. Shah was doing the same with the boys, and Ellie couldn't help trying to count along his line, to try to work out whom she'd be partnering. If she was the fourth smallest, then . . . Toby, Nick, James . . . Oliver? She felt her shoulders slump a little with disappointment as Mr. Shah lined Oliver up behind James as the fourth smallest of the boys. Oh, no! Oliver Stafford was just about the only person in the whole class that Ellie didn't really like! He was the most arrogant boy she'd ever met. Was she really going to have to partner with him? Oliver Stafford was the kind of person who'd trip her up onstage at The Royal Opera House just for a laugh, she knew it!

Matt followed Oliver in the line of boys. Ellie held her breath while her teacher thought for a moment—and then swapped her and Megan in line.

"So Megan's fourth and Ellie's fifth..." Ms. Wells said to herself, and then moved farther up the line.

Ellie felt a grin spread over her face, and gave a thumbs-up sign to Matt across the room. He'd seen the swap and was beaming at her.

"Ellie Brown, you lucky thing! Looks like *I'm* going to be dancing with Oliver now," Megan whispered, rolling her eyes.

"Sorry, Megan," Ellie replied, with a sympathetic smile. "You don't mind too much, do you?"

Megan shook her head. "No, not really. Dancing with Oliver Stafford might make me look better!" she whispered back with a wry grin. "He can be a pain—but there's no denying he can dance!"

After they had all been paired up, Ms. Wells and Mr. Shah spoke quietly together for a few seconds and then called out for Kate and Nick to come into the center, along with Isabelle and Alex.

Ellie felt her heart begin to thump. The teachers must already be trying to decide who the central couples were going to be.

Mr. Shah set a short sequence and asked the four of them to dance it, while he and Ms. Wells made notes.

And then Ellie and Matt were called into the center, along with Grace and Danny. They were asked to dance the same series of steps as a foursome.

"And . . . step . . . and turn . . . and *glissade, glissade*," Ms. Wells told them.

Ellie could feel her teacher's eyes upon her as she tried to dance her very best.

"Lovely," Ms. Wells said approvingly at the end. "Matt and Ellie, could you stay where you are, please?" She consulted with Mr. Shah. "Justin and Lara, if you could swap places with Danny and Grace, please?"

Ellie tried not to show how thrilled she felt as she remained in the center of the studio with Matt. *Does that mean . . . ? Could it be?* She hardly dared think the words. Was Ms. Wells seriously considering her and Matt as one of the central couples?

Sophie was winking at her from the sidelines, and giving her a thumbs-up. Lara, too, was smiling broadly at Ellie as she walked into the center with Justin. But Grace . . . *Oh, no.* Ellie's spirits sagged as she caught sight of her friend's expression. Having been sent out of the center and back to the sidelines, Grace looked as if she'd been slapped right in the face.

Dear Diary,
    We had our first Grand Défilé

rehearsal with the boys this afternoon! We'll be rehearsing with them every Wednesday and Friday now, until the end-of-year performances. It was awesome—AND Ms. Wells and Mr. Shah seem to be seriously considering Matt and me as one of the central couples! They said they haven't finally decided on the two exact couples yet, but hey, I really feel like I'm in the running. YAY!

Everyone is just BUZZING with excitement wondering who's going to get the starring roles in the center. Except Grace, that is . . . She told me she thinks she's probably already been rejected for the center—and she switched her cell phone off tonight, because she knew that her mom would call and ask her about how the first rehearsal class went. I guess she just didn't want to talk about it with her.

She sure is working hard, too. She went off to do more dance practice after dinner—and she only stopped when one of the house-mothers sent her back to the dorm because it was less than an hour until lights-out.

Chapter 4

On Friday afternoon, Ellie could barely swallow her tuck fast enough, she was so eager to go and get ready for their second ballet rehearsal. She was trying not to dwell on it too much, but it was almost impossible to stop herself from thinking over and over again, *Will Ms. Wells and Mr. Shah have chosen their central couples by now?* Oh, Ellie hoped so! She could hardly bear to wait another five minutes to find out!

There was a knot in her tummy as she sprayed her hair carefully into place in front of her mirror. Then she looked down at her watch and gulped. "Come on," she said to Grace. "Rehearsal starts in two minutes. We'd better hurry."

Grace was still pushing bobby pins into her hair to keep her bun in place. Then she grimaced at her reflection. "Oh, it's still wonky," she complained, reaching up to undo the bun.

"Oh, no, you don't," Ellie said, grabbing her friend by the hand. They'd be there for ages if she let Grace start doing and undoing her hair, as she had been all week. Besides, Grace's hair looked as immaculate as ever, in Ellie's eyes. "We don't have time for you to start all over again," Ellie said firmly before Grace could protest. "And anyway, your bun isn't the slightest bit wonky. It's fine, absolutely fine."

Grace yanked her hand out of Ellie's to straighten her bed covers as she went past her bed.

Ellie, with a rather guilty glance back at her own unmade bed, promised herself quickly that she'd figure her mess out after class. Right now, she could think of nothing else but the rehearsal.

She wasn't the only one. Every other girl in the dorm seemed to be talking about it!

"So who do we all think the central couples will be?" Sophie asked the group as they all ran down the steps together toward the studio where the rehearsal was to be held. "My money's on the teachers picking you and Matt, Ellie," she added, grinning at Ellie. "I thought you were really good at the last rehearsal."

"Thanks, Soph," Ellie said. She *sooo* hoped Sophie was right! "But I thought Lara and Justin danced really well together, too," she added.

"Justin would make anybody look good," said Lara modestly. "He is so brilliant."

"I guess we're just going to have to wait and see," Ellie said. *As long as we don't have to wait too long*, she added grimly in her head. The anticipation was starting to drive her crazy!

• • • •

"Good afternoon, everyone," Ms. Wells said, as she and Mr. Shah came into the studio. Ellie and the other Year 7 students paused in their warm-up routines to curtsy and bow and reply, "Good afternoon," in one voice.

"Carry on with your warm-ups," Mr. Shah told them. "And once you've finished, we'll start our rehearsal. We're hoping to decide the central couples by the end of this afternoon's session."

Without another word, every student in the room turned back to the barre diligently and worked through their warm-up exercises. Ellie had to be careful not to rush through them, she was so excited. *But now would be a truly awful time to get an injury or cramp by not warming up all my muscles correctly*, she reminded herself, carefully stretching out her hamstrings one by one.

A few minutes later, the room was silent with anticipation.

"All right," said Mr. Shah, consulting a piece of paper. "So, the smallest couple—Bryony and Toby—will be leading everyone else in. Bryony and Toby, could you two come out here, please?"

Clearly delighted to be the first ones onstage, a beaming Bryony and Toby walked toward the center, and Mr. Shah ran through the choreography with them. "You'll come together, like so . . ." he said, "and then, facing each other, I want you to do *balancés en avant* and *en arrière*, forward and backward." He demonstrated quickly with Ms. Wells. "Step forward, arms through *bras bas* to first, and on to first *arabesque* . . ."

Everybody watched as the teachers went through the steps together, combining the *balancé*—or rocking step—with a *temps levé* in first *arabesque*.

"And then you'll separate again, to stand here . . . and here . . ." Mr. Shah went on, positioning Bryony and Toby opposite each other, one on either side of the studio, ". . . in a *dégagé* pose." Bryony and Toby obediently stood in *dégagé*, with their front feet stretched out.

"So, first couple, could you try that from the top, please?" Ms. Wells asked. "Starting positions, please . . . And come together . . . And into your *balancés*." She watched critically as Bryony and Toby followed her directions. "So you're starting *en croisé*, remember, arms *demi-seconde* for the girls, and *bras bas* for the boys. That's it."

Ellie and the other students looked on as Bryony and Toby went through the steps before separating once again to stand in *dégagé* together.

"Very nice." Ms. Wells smiled. She looked over at Mr. Shah and they nodded. "Looks good. Now, following close behind will be . . . Kate and Nick, our second couple," she went on. "So, if you would do the same, please?"

Kate and Nick danced the same series of steps as shown, before going to stand in *dégagé* at either side of the studio.

"The third couple will be Alice and James," Mr. Shah went on. "Same thing: Alice following close behind Kate, James close behind Nick . . . Come together . . . Dance here . . . Separate—and over to your respective sides . . . Good! Everybody see the idea?"

"Yes," the class chorused.

Megan and Oliver were next, then Ellie and Matt. Ellie tried to remember everything she'd ever learned about *balancés* before—taking care not to tilt too far back in the first *arabesque*, and remembering to lean forward from her waist, not her hips, when she was moving *en arrière*, the backward part of the rocking step.

"Very nice," Ms. Wells said approvingly as Ellie and Matt finished the movement and took their places at the side of the stage. Ellie smiled across at Matt. She loved dancing with him— and she knew that they'd both danced well just then.

The rehearsal went on, with every couple practicing their entrances, their steps, and then their retreat to the sides. Then, once all the girls were on one side in *dégagé*, and the boys on the other, Ms. Wells and Mr. Shah conferred for a moment in the center.

"Right, we're going to try out for the central couples again now," Ms. Wells told them. "We do have a shortlist, and we have finalized the choreography, so we'll see how it goes today. Kate and Nick, can we have you in the middle first, please? And Lara and Justin—you, too."

Lara's pale skin flushed with pleasure as she stepped forward into the center of the studio. Kate, too, looked thrilled at the honor. Ms. Wells and Mr. Shah put them in a square formation, then talked both couples through a series of steps where each couple traveled diagonally across the square.

The whole movement lasted no more than a minute or so, but even so, Ellie knew what prestige it carried: to be one of the four students chosen to solo in the *Grand Défilé* . . . Wow.

Isabelle and Alex were called into the center next, and Ellie and Matt. Ellie's heart thumped as she took up her position next to Isabelle, facing Matt in the square formation, and she felt her skin prickle with excitement.

"Ready? And one, two, hold three, extend four," Ms. Wells called out. "Arms, Alex! Single, single, close . . . Nice fifth, Ellie, let your wrists go, Isabelle . . ."

Ellie could think of nothing but following her teacher's instructions to the letter, trying to impress Ms. Wells and Mr. Shah with her precision and control.

"One, two, turn and stay, use the floor, Matt . . . and close. Very nice," Ms. Wells finished. "You four can go back to your places now." Once again, she and Mr. Shah bent their heads together to discuss the students, and Ellie watched them like a hawk. She wished she could lip-read!

Ms. Wells called Megan and Oliver, and then Grace and Danny. Grace's face was frozen as her name was called, and she immediately clutched a hand to her chest as if she were worried her heart was about to thump its way out of there, Ellie thought. *Come on, Grace, keep your cool,* she urged her friend mentally. *Show them just how good we all know you can be!*

Once again, the square was formed and the four students went through the routine. Grace was performing her steps well, Ellie observed. But there was not a single glimmer of pleasure in her eyes, she saw with dismay. Grace's face seemed hard. Oh, Ellie so wished that Grace could just loosen up a little and enjoy her performing.

Once Grace's group had finished the routine, Ms. Wells and Mr. Shah went into their usual huddle. This time, the discussion went on for a long time, and the teachers seemed to be in some disagreement. Mr. Shah seemed to be looking at Matt as he muttered to Ms. Wells. And Ms. Wells then seemed to be looking at Megan as she replied.

Ellie felt her face flood with heat. Oh, what if they were going to change some of the partners? What if Mr. Shah thought Matt had danced well enough to be picked as a central dancer—but that she, Ellie, hadn't? What if they decided to put Matt with Megan instead?

A hand was squeezing hers, and Ellie looked around to see Lara's fingers around her own. Ellie squeezed back.

"I can't bear the suspense," Lara whispered. "What do you think they're saying?"

Grace answered before Ellie. "They're saying how awful I was, probably," she mumbled, a muscle twitching in her jaw. "Ms. Wells looked straight at me just then—did you see?"

Ellie shook her head. "They don't think you were awful—they

shortlisted you, Grace," Ellie reminded her firmly. "You were good, and so was Danny."

"Okay," Ms. Wells said after a few more moments. "We'd like to see Ellie and Matt again, please. And Grace and Danny. Could you all come to the center?"

Ellie's heart stepped up a gear. Grace looked as if she was about to pass out. What did this mean? Ellie wondered, her mind racing. Were they thinking of casting the four of them as the central couples? Or had they already selected one couple for sure, and this was to choose the second couple? She gulped as she took her place opposite Matt. Was this a showdown between her and her best friend?

Matt winked reassuringly at Ellie, and she smiled gratefully back at him. Thank *goodness* she had Matt to calm her nerves. And thank goodness Ms. Wells hadn't decided to make her swap back with Megan, after all!

"Good luck," she whispered quickly to Grace, but Grace didn't seem to hear her. She was smoothing her hair back agitatedly as if her very performance depended upon it.

"And . . . off we go," Mr. Shah said. "Pull up, and three, four, both legs working, Grace, use the floor . . ."

Ellie could almost hear her heart thumping over the sound of their ballet shoes swishing on the studio floor. *Smile!* she ordered herself. *Focus! Clean, precise movements!*

"And . . . thank you," Mr. Shah said as they finished the

routine. He looked over at Ms. Wells, and they returned to their huddle. Both were nodding now as they spoke, and Ellie felt as if her insides were being squeezed, so nervous did she feel. She'd been concentrating so hard, she had no idea how Grace and Danny had danced. She thought she'd managed to dance well herself, though—but would the teachers agree?

She looked at Grace, whose eyes were fixed steadfastly upon the teachers. All color had drained from her friend's face.

"Right," said Ms. Wells, turning back to the studio. "Sorry to put you through such suspense! The first couple we've chosen is Lara and Justin."

A gasp went up from Lara; she clearly hadn't been expecting to be picked. Her face wreathed in smiles, she ran over to hug Justin. "Can you believe it? This is just so grand, isn't it?" she whispered excitedly, and loudly.

A chuckle went around the room, but Ellie couldn't even smile she was so tense herself. *So chances are, the second couple is either going to be me and Matt—or Grace and Danny . . .* she thought. She grabbed Grace's hand and held it tightly.

"And our second couple is going to be . . . Ellie and Matt," said Mr. Shah.

Wow. Wow! WOW! Ellie's mouth fell open as she heard her name. She'd been picked! She'd actually been picked as one of the star dancers in her year—to perform on the main stage at The Royal Opera House! How unbelievable was that?!

"Well done, you four," Ms. Wells concluded with a smile.

Matt rushed over, picked Ellie up, and swung her around, laughing. Ellie felt dazed with happiness. "Omigosh!" she kept saying over and over again. "Omigosh, Matt. It's us! It's really us!"

But then she caught sight of Grace's expression, and stopped dead. For Grace looked as though her world had just fallen apart. Her mouth trembled in a way that Ellie knew meant she was close to tears. Ellie disentangled herself from Matt and went over to her friend. "Oh, Grace," she said, hugging her. "Are you all right?"

Grace's face was ashen. "What am I going to tell my mum?" was all she could say.

•　　　•　　　•　　　•

At the end of the rehearsal, Grace stayed behind to talk to Ms. Wells. Lara grabbed Ellie as they went out of the studio together, and they both whooped and cheered. "Come on, let's call our moms," Ellie suggested, rushing toward the stairs. "I can't wait to tell mine!"

As soon as they were back in the dorm, Ellie ran straight to get her cell phone and dialed her mom's work number before she'd even gotten changed.

"Mom . . . Hi, it's me!" she said breathlessly, when her mom picked up. "You'll never guess what . . . I got picked for one of the main roles in the *Grand Défilé*! Me and Lara!"

"Oh, honey," her mom gasped, "that's wonderful!" She sounded every bit as thrilled as Ellie.

"I know. I know! I can't believe it!" Ellie said, feeling a huge surge of joy all over again as she told her mom all about the rehearsal and being chosen.

"Our tickets for both the Friday night Linbury performance and the final matinee arrived just today," Ellie's mom told her afterward. "And honey, I'm going to be the proudest mom in the whole Royal Opera House!"

As Ellie hung up her phone, she could hear Lara, who had the bed next to her in the dorm, having pretty much the exact same conversation with *her* mom. "Love you, too, Mum, bye," Lara said, hanging up with bright eyes.

Grace came into the dorm just then, and slowly got her phone out, too.

Ellie looked at her sympathetically. "Are you calling home?" she asked.

Grace shook her head and slung her phone back into her desk drawer. "I'll phone her later," she said, turning away to flick some lint off her leotard.

Ellie realized with a pang that Grace had actually been switching her cell phone *off*, rather than dialing a number.

She watched her friend busying herself by straightening up the books on her shelf. She felt desperately sorry for her. It was clear that Grace didn't feel up to speaking to her mom about the casting for the *Grand Défilé* right now. Ellie couldn't help wondering who was going to be more disappointed that Grace hadn't been picked for a main part: Grace or her mom?

• • • •

After supper that evening, Ellie and some of the others were in the dorm sorting out their ballet uniforms and schoolbooks for the following day. They wouldn't have time later, since their favorite TV show was on that evening, and it went on until just a few minutes before lights-out.

Mrs. Hall put her head around the door. "Is Grace in here?" she asked, and then smiled as she spotted her. "Oh, hello there, Grace—your mum's been on the phone. Could you give her a call back as soon as possible, please?"

"Um . . . Yes, sure," Grace replied.

When Mrs. Hall had left the dorm again, Grace went back to sorting out the books that she needed.

Ellie watched as Grace tried to smooth out a crease on the cover of her geography exercise book. She then piled the books together: biology textbook at the bottom, because that was the biggest, then her geography and history textbooks, followed by her notebooks—and finally, the novel they were reading in English. She spent a little while straightening all the book spines so that the pile was neatly perfect.

Ellie sighed in sympathy. Grace was so obviously putting off having to call her mom!

Then Grace opened her pencil tin and started sharpening her pencils, even though Ellie could see that none of them were blunt.

"Um . . . Grace," she said tentatively. "Don't you think you should call your mom back, now?"

Grace's shoulders stiffened at Ellie's words. There was a small silence, except for the scraping sound of her pencil sharpener. And then Grace sighed and lined her pencils up neatly in the tin before putting the tin on top of the books. "I suppose I'd better get it over and done with," she muttered, switching on her cell phone and dialing.

Ellie then remembered that she still needed to find the sheets of paper on which she'd written the details of her history prep. She'd unearthed one of them from under her bed, but the other one seemed to have vanished off the planet. As she searched frantically through her drawers, she couldn't help overhearing Grace's conversation.

"Hi, it's me . . ." Grace began. "Sorry I didn't call earlier . . . The cell phone reception can be really bad here sometimes . . ."

Ellie frowned at Grace's untruth, and tried to stop herself from listening in—but it was almost impossible.

". . . I'm partners with Danny, which is really good because he's . . . What?" There was a pause. "Oh, no, we're not one of the central couples, no. . . . Well, only two girls got picked and . . . Well, I *am* with Danny, who's one of the best boys, so . . ." Grace sighed. "Mum, I don't know why he didn't get picked, either, but . . ."

Grace's voice was getting lower and lower and she was hunching down over the phone. Ellie could see her friend's ears turning red as the conversation went on and she felt a stab of anger at Grace's mom. She clearly wasn't very pleased with the news that Grace hadn't got a starring role in the *Grand Défilé*—which wasn't fair.

Grace started picking at a little scab on her arm. "Well, look, that's the way it is," she said in a tight voice. "I've got to go now. I'll tell you more about it this weekend, okay?"

Aha! The missing piece of history prep was stuffed in her physics book. Ellie smoothed it out hastily and put it with the rest of her history things.

Grace's voice had become a little higher-pitched. "What do you mean? Why?" she was saying, and Ellie glanced over. Grace was picking at her arm so agitatedly that the scab opened up and started to bleed. "All right, bye then," she said, and hung up the call.

"Are you okay?" Ellie asked. "What did she say?"

Grace jumped up. "Oh, no! Now look what I've done!" she said, ignoring Ellie's question.

Ellie looked to see that a tiny fleck of blood had landed on Grace's duvet cover. "Never mind," she said. "You can hardly see it. It'll come out in the wash."

"It won't," Grace said. "I'll have to rinse it right now, or it'll stain." She put her pile of schoolbooks down on the floor and started pulling her quilt cover off.

Ellie watched Grace hurry into the bathroom with it. She left her own books and went after her friend.

Grace scrubbed furiously at the tiny red speck until it had disappeared.

"I take it your mom wasn't thrilled by your news," Ellie said after a few moments' silence.

Grace shook her head, squeezing the water out of her quilt cover. She didn't look Ellie in the eye as she replied. "No," she said quietly. "She was really disappointed. She even suggested that I not come home this weekend, so as to get more practice in."

"What?" Ellie asked in disbelief. Grace went home to her mom's practically every single weekend. She hardly ever stayed at school.

Grace nodded. "She says I should be practicing every chance I get so that even though my part is small, I'll still be outstanding," she told Ellie heavily. "And given that the show isn't on until the very end of term, she's basically said that I shouldn't come home at all this half-term!"

Dear Diary,
    Poor Grace! It's almost as if she's being punished by her mom. I can't believe that her

mom has pretty much banned her from coming home until the end of term! Grace is really going to miss her friends at home, and her dog, too. It is so unfair, if you ask me.

I hereby vow to make sure Grace Tennant has lots of fun on weekends while she's at school—and not let her just practice until she drops, like her mom seems to expect. There's a shopping trip to Sheen planned for Sunday and I'm going to make sure she comes with me and the other girls. Even if I have to drag her along! One way or another, I'll get Grace to let her hair down over the weekend—literally!

Chapter 5

Sunday! It's Sunday . . . Ellie remembered with a smile, as she gradually came awake. Sunday was the only day of the week during term-time when the students could have a bit of a lie-in, as they had their usual morning ballet class on Saturdays. Ellie's eyes were still closed, but she could feel light on her face as it came creeping into the dorm. It must be sunny outside. Better and better! And they were going to Sheen, the small town nearest The Royal Ballet Lower School, that morning for shopping and smoothies and unwinding . . . Bliss.

Ellie rolled over and opened her eyes. "Hey, Grace," she began, and then stopped. She sat up and stared over at her friend's bed. The covers were pulled up and smoothed out—and the bed was empty.

She must have gotten up already, and gone to the bathroom, Ellie thought, dragging back the curtain near her bed so that she could peek outside. She'd been right. It looked gorgeous out there—blue sky, and not a single cloud on the horizon. Perfect. The sun streamed right into the dorm where the curtain was open and Ellie leaned back against her pillow, basking in its warmth.

She decided to read another chapter of the book they had been assigned for English.

It was only when Mrs. Hall came to rouse them all with her "Good morning" wake-up call ten minutes later, that Ellie started to wonder what had happened to Grace. Was she really still in the bathroom, or had she gone someplace else?

Just then, Grace arrived back at the dorm, rosy-cheeked and in her sweat suit.

"Hi there," Ellie called out curiously, putting her book back on her bedside table. "Where've you been?"

Grace unzipped her red sweat-suit jacket, and wiped the hair out of her eyes. "Just thought I'd get in some extra practice before breakfast," she said, getting her towel and shower things from her cupboard. "I set my alarm early—it didn't disturb any of you, did it?"

Sophie was sitting up in bed and staring at Grace as if she were completely crazy. "Practice for what? The end-of-year performances?" she asked in astonishment. "But we've got weeks to go before they start."

Grace's flushed cheeks turned a deeper pink. "Well, you know, I just want to do my best," she said. Then, before anyone could say anything else, she went to shower, leaving the others to exchange surprised glances. Ballet before breakfast? No one could possibly say that Grace wasn't taking the performances anything less than seriously.

•   •   •   •

After breakfast, Ellie and her friends got ready to go out to Sheen. As Ellie had guessed, persuading Grace to come along wasn't a very easy task.

"But I don't want to!" she said when Ellie tried to talk her into it. "I'd rather hang out here."

"Do some more practice, you mean," Sophie said. Ellie knew that Sophie was only teasing Grace, but Grace instantly went on the defensive.

"And what's wrong with that?" she asked. "So what if I do want to practice? It's not a crime, is it? We are all students at The Royal Ballet School—we're *supposed* to be practicing ballet, remember?"

Sophie held up her hands and made a "Whoa!" kind of face. "All right, keep your hair on," she said, shrugging on a denim jacket. "I was only joking, Grace."

"Come on, Grace," Ellie pleaded. "You haven't been to Sheen for forever. It'll be really fun. And last term we found this little café that does the best smoothies on earth . . ." There was a pause and Ellie knew she almost had her. "Last time I had raspberry, banana, and peach flavor . . ." she added temptingly, knowing that raspberries were Grace's very favorite fruit.

Grace weakened and smiled at Ellie. "You got me," she admitted. "Let me just do my hair and I'll be ready."

"Minibus leaves in five minutes," Lara reminded them, going off to brush her teeth.

Ellie picked up a shoulder bag and stuffed her purse, sunglasses, and cell phone inside, plus a bunch of letters to mail to her friends Phoebe and Bethany in Oxford and her grandparents in Chicago. She gave her own hair a quick brush, bundled it up into a ponytail, and then tucked it in her favorite pink baseball cap. Done.

She slung her bag on one shoulder and waited for Grace, who was combing out her hair. Ellie stared as she watched Grace comb one small section at a time, painstakingly checking each one as she moved her way around her head.

Lara came back, grabbed a jacket and her bag, and looked over questioningly. "Should we go?" she asked.

"I'm ready," Sophie said, shuffling her feet into some pink flip-flops and tucking her purse into a pocket of her denim skirt.

"I'll be two seconds," Grace said, still combing. "Ellie, go on with the others if you want. I'll catch up." She began scraping her hair back from her face.

"Come on, Grace," Sophie called over. "You look gorgeous already. The minibus will leave without us if we don't hurry."

"I'll wait with Grace," Ellie told her. "You two go ahead and we'll see you on the bus."

She stood there while Grace combed her hair back, and then fastened it up in a ponytail with a clip.

Ellie glanced down at her watch anxiously—they really were going to miss the minibus if they didn't hurry. She waited as Grace put her brush and comb away neatly, and carefully brushed out the creases on her duvet where she'd been sitting.

Finally Ellie could stand it no longer. She knew Grace wasn't particularly eager to go shopping, but this was ridiculous! "Come on," she pleaded. "We really do have to go *now* or they'll all go without us."

Grace jumped, almost as if she'd forgotten Ellie was there. "Sorry," she said. "I'll just—"

"That can wait, Grace—but the minibus won't!" Ellie interrupted. She grabbed Grace's bag in one hand and Grace's arm in the other, and pulled her toward the door.

"But my—no, wait!" Grace said, wriggling her fingers out of Ellie's. She went back to her bed and brushed a couple of stray hairs off the pillow. "Okay," she said, running back to Ellie. "Let's go."

Ellie and Grace ran downstairs and out to the front of the school where the minibus engine had already started. *Honestly,* Ellie thought as they raced over to the minibus, waving frantically. *What is going on with Grace lately? All this fussing and checking, and wanting everything to be just so . . .* She bit her lip. She'd thought Grace was just becoming more finicky, but now . . . It seemed to be more than that. What could it be?

Mr. Lewis, one of the teachers taking the students to Sheen, was just about to shut the bus doors but luckily spotted them *just* in time. "You just made it," he told them laughingly as they scrambled on board. "By a whisker!"

• • • •

Ellie, Sophie, and Lara had developed something of a ritual for their Sunday shopping trips. They went into the clothing shops first to try on a few new outfits, even though they could hardly ever afford to buy anything. Then they'd stroll along to a gift shop they loved that sold really cool cards and trinkets, and then they'd visit the large drugstore to try on perfume and lipstick. And then finally, when their legs were starting to ache from all the walking, they went to their favorite streetside café for hot chocolate when the day was chilly or smoothies when it was warm.

Grace was a little quiet at first, but after Sophie had entertained them all by trying on a display of sun hats and making silly faces with each one, Ellie realized that Grace was starting to laugh and joke along with the rest of them, and seemed more like her usual self. Thank goodness she'd talked her into coming, Ellie thought as Grace giggled helplessly at Sophie's clowning. Even prima ballerinas needed some serious time-out.

After they'd bought everything they needed, Ellie and her friends made their way to the café.

Grace took her first sip of her raspberry, peach, and banana smoothie. A look of bliss came over her face and she leaned back into her armchair. "You were right," she told Ellie. "Absolutely the best smoothie I've ever tasted, too."

Sophie, who had gone for a strawberry and banana one, nodded. "I think we're going to need one of these every single Sunday until the end-of-year performances," she said. "From here on in, it's just going to get tougher, what with exams to review for, too."

"You're not wrong," Lara groaned, using a long spoon to eat the thick blueberry and banana smoothie she'd chosen. "Nose to the grindstone—and toes to the barre!"

"I hope we get a chance to see the other years' performances," Ellie said. After much agonizing, she'd gone for an orange and mango smoothie, which tasted utterly divine. "Especially the graduates," she added.

"I just want to get on that stage myself!" said Sophie. "It's all right for you, Ellie and Lara, you've already danced at The Royal Opera House when you did *The Nutcracker* at Christmas—but Grace and I haven't, and I'm just itching to see what it's like."

Grace wasn't saying anything, Ellie noticed. She was concentrating on making a tower of coins from her change—largest on the bottom, smallest on top. The smile had vanished from her face with talk of the end-of-year performances.

"What's everyone planning to do later?" Ellie asked, in order to change the subject as much as anything.

Sophie finished her smoothie with a loud slurp. "Half a ton of prep, unfortunately," she said. She stretched her bare leg out from under the table. "Although I might be tempted outside to sunbathe instead, if anyone fancies joining me in the garden?"

"Maybe later," Ellie agreed. "I haven't started my English essay yet. Has anybody else?"

Sophie snorted. "'Course I haven't!" she said. "And as for all those math equations we've got to do for tomorrow . . ." She made a face. "How will I ever perfect my tan with all this prep?"

"Looks like we'll all have to be pale until the summer holidays," Lara sighed. "Anyway, why are we talking about schoolwork? It's putting me off my smoothie. Oh, yes! I've been meaning to ask you guys . . . you know that bit in the Holubetz we were doing last Monday, the bit where—"

Grace's fingers jerked suddenly, and her neat tower of coins toppled over. Coins went bouncing all over the floor. "Oh, no!" she wailed, crawling under the table to collect them up.

Ellie bent down to help her. "I guess we'd better make tracks," she said, noticing the café clock up on the wall. "Here you are, Grace," she went on, handing over the coins she'd picked up. "Let's go and get our prep over and done with. At least then we don't have to feel too guilty about watching a movie together this evening."

"Suppose you're right," Lara agreed with a sigh. She spooned up the last of her smoothie. "Okay—French books, here I come!"

•   •   •   •

Back at school, while Ellie, Lara, and Sophie got themselves organized to do their prep, Grace changed into her leotard, pulled on her sweat suit and sneakers, and announced she was off to the studio.

"Ballet shoes, towel, water bottle, tissues . . ." she checked off as she placed each item into her bag. "See you guys later," she called, moving over to the door. Then she opened up her ballet bag again. "Ballet shoes, towel, water bottle, tissues . . ." she reeled off to herself.

"Are they all still in there, Grace? Or did anything fall out between your bed and the doorway?" Sophie joked.

Grace looked a little taken aback at the question. "Pardon?" she asked.

"I mean, you just checked you had everything when you were standing by your bed, then you walked to the door and checked it all again," Sophie observed with a grin. "Honestly, Grace, your memory must be like a sieve—just like mine," she added cheerfully.

Ellie's heart sank as she saw that tight, pinched, defensive expression return to Grace's face. "I was just making sure I had everything," she said. "Nothing wrong with that, is there?"

"No. Of course not," Sophie said quickly. "I was just saying that—"

But Grace had already left the room.

"I was just saying that it was odd," Sophie finished in a thoughtful voice, staring at the empty space where Grace had been. "But hey. What do I know?"

Dear Diary,
   I'm curled up in the common room writing this—Soph's just about to put on a movie for us to watch. I'm feeling very proud

of myself. I got my English essay done AND all my math prep, too. Darn it, I'm good!

Grace hasn't been around much today. She seemed to cheer up when we were out of school this morning but then, as soon as we started talking about the end-of-year performances, she clammed up and got all twitchy again. And she practiced for ages this afternoon. She's doing her prep now in the dorm rather than hanging out with us. I did ask her to come and watch the movie—and Lara did, too, AND Sophie—but Grace says she wants to catch up on her prep before tomorrow.

I'm a little worried about her, to be honest. I just don't understand this new thing she's got about looking perfect the whole time. It's not like her at all. And suddenly, everything with her has to be just so—she keeps checking things over and over to make sure they're how she wants them. And then there's all this extra ballet practice she's putting in . . .

I don't know—I'm just hoping that she'll snap out of it soon.

6

"Achoo! Achoo!"

"Bless you," Ellie said as Lara rubbed her red, watery eyes. "And bless you again."

Lara blew her nose and groaned. "It's just the worst thing about summer," she complained. "Hay fever every year. *ACHOO!"*

It was the following Monday afternoon and Ellie and her friends had come out into the school gardens to eat their tuck before their character dancing class. Poor Lara had been sneezing all afternoon, and had missed half the English class that the Year 7 students had just had, because she'd gone to the sick room to get some allergy medication.

"Who's your partner in character again?" Sophie asked. "Alex, isn't it? Well, I hope he's got some tissues with him, otherwise—"

"All right, all right!" Isabelle put in hurriedly with a delicate shudder. "Sophie, please. I don't want to know what you are thinking."

Ellie finished her granola bar and scrunched up the wrapper in her hand. "Yum," she said, jumping up. "I'm going to get changed for character class, I think. Anyone coming?"

"Me," Lara said, blowing her nose again. "I wish those tablets would hurry up and start working. The last thing I feel like doing is dancing right now."

"Come on," Ellie said, reaching down a hand and pulling Lara to her feet. "Are you coming, Grace?"

Grace nodded and got up, too, brushing a few stray blades of grass off her legs. "Have I got any on my skirt?" she asked Ellie, turning around so that Ellie could see.

"Nope," Ellie said. "Come on, let's go in. I'm really excited to learn more of the Polish dance. I've been practicing what we've learned so far in my head all week."

Grace was still brushing down her skirt, even though there was absolutely nothing on it. "I can't stand having grass on my clothes," she said when she realized Ellie and Lara were waiting for her.

Sophie got to her feet now, too, along with Kate. "I think you've got it all now, Grace," Sophie said, swallowing her last mouthful.

"Okay," Grace said uncertainly. "If you're sure . . ."

"One hundred percent," Sophie said, grabbing her by the arm and walking off to school. "Off we go!"

•   •   •   •

After changing into their character dancing uniforms and making their way to the studio, Ellie and the other girls took off their red sweat-suit tops and began warming up. Likewise, the boys took off their blue sweat suits to reveal their ballet uniform of white top and blue shorts underneath.

Matt came over to say hi and began warming up nearby. He looked tired, Ellie thought. "Everything okay?" she asked him.

Matt was lifting each shoulder in turn and rolling his neck around to warm up the muscles. "Yeah," he said. "Just wondering how we're going to cram in all this prep and rehearsals and exam revision. I'm behind already, and it's only the second week of term."

"I know," Ellie said, sinking into a *plié*. "I haven't done my chemistry assignment for tomorrow yet, have you? Or my French comprehension. And we've got all those map symbols to learn for geography . . ."

"Exactly," Matt said. He began swinging his arms around from side to side, shaking them to loosen them up. Then he smiled his more usual smile. "We are so going to need a break after all of this. When term's over, I'm just going to sleep for a whole week."

"Part of me wants to do that already," Ellie agreed with a laugh. She began warming up next to Grace. "What a luxury, eh, Grace? A week of sleep—no ballet practice, no prep . . ." Ellie paused, expecting Grace to agree with her, but her friend was clearly not listening.

Grace stopped warming up to peer closely at the wall mirror in front of her. Then she started pulling her bun loose.

"What are you doing?" Ellie asked.

"I hadn't realized how messy my hair was," Grace said, frowning anxiously at her reflection. She tugged her hair pins out so frantically that several of them clattered to the floor. "Why didn't somebody tell me it was so messy? Why didn't you *tell* me, Ellie?"

"But it *wasn't* messy," Ellie protested. She sank down into another *plié*, and leaned over to pick up some of the bobby pins from her position. "I would have told you if it was messy, but it wasn't—it looked fine, Grace."

Grace's mouth was set in a tight line as she shook her hair loose, then began scraping it back to put it into a bun again.

"Do you want a hand?" Ellie asked tentatively. Grace seemed really upset!

"No, thank you," Grace said, pushing her pins back in with real force.

Ouch! Ellie thought, as she went back to her warm-up. *That must really hurt. Grace, what are you doing?*

"Oh, it still isn't right!" Grace wailed a moment later. "What am I going to do?"

"Grace, it looks absolutely fine," Ellie told her earnestly, as she stretched over her leg at the barre. "As long as it's not dangling down in your eyes then it doesn't matter so much anyway. It's not like we're about to go onstage or anything, is it?"

Ms. O'Connor came in just then. With an anxious squeak, Grace pushed in the rest of her pins and went back to warming up. But it was clear she was distracted. She kept peering into the mirror and checking her hair for stray ends.

Ellie couldn't help glancing uneasily at her friend. Grace

seemed more fretful than ever today. And she looked exhausted, too, Ellie thought, spotting telltale dark circles under Grace's eyes. Stretching her arms out above her head, Ellie pulled on each wrist to lengthen the stretch a little farther. It was too bad Grace's mom had made such a silly decision about Grace not coming home over the weekends. Grace clearly needed a break.

Ms. O'Connor clapped her hands for attention. "Hello, everyone," she greeted them. "Has everybody finished warming up? Good. Before we start our class, I thought you might like to know what you'll be wearing for your end-of-year performance."

Ellie turned to look at once. Ms. O'Connor was holding up a coat hanger in each hand, from which hung two different outfits. "This one, obviously, is for the girls," Ms. O'Connor said, lifting one outfit a little higher. "And this is for the boys. What does everyone think?"

"Nice," a couple of girls said approvingly. Ellie really liked the girls' costume. It consisted of a white peasant blouse with short puffed sleeves and a scoop neck, and a full black skirt with several red stripes around the bottom, plus a white frilly petticoat. The boys' outfit didn't look half as interesting. They'd be wearing black trousers and a white top—but at least they had a red cummerbund.

"Girls, you'll also be wearing pink tights and a red sash," Ms. O'Connor went on, hanging the two outfits on the barre behind her. "I'll leave those there for class so you can feel even more inspired while you're dancing," she added with a smile.

"What do you think?" Ellie asked Grace. "Sweet, aren't they?"

She turned back to her friend to see that Grace was still staring intently into the mirror. She hadn't even seen the costumes yet; she was still worrying about her hair. Ellie bit her lip. She really had to think of something to snap Grace out of her weirdness. It was starting to get out of hand. But what?

• • • •

That evening, Ellie was about to call her mom when Grace passed by—on her way to do yet more extra dance practice. Ellie sighed. Grace really needed to give herself a break!

Suddenly, Ellie had an idea. Maybe *she* could give Grace a break—in Oxford! She quickly dialed home.

Her mom picked up almost immediately and, once they'd caught up a little, Ellie pressed on with her idea. "Mom," she began, checking that nobody was within earshot, "would it be okay if I come home this weekend—and bring a friend with me?" she asked.

"Of course, honey," her mom said at once. "It would be so great to see you. And whom do you want to bring?"

"I was thinking of asking Grace," Ellie replied. "She seems kind of uptight these days. I think she could stand to get away from school for a while."

"Grace?" said her mom, sounding a little surprised. "Doesn't Grace go home most weekends, anyway?" she asked. "Or am I thinking of someone else?"

"No, you're right, she does usually go home," Ellie replied. "Only . . . well, if I tell you, you can't say anything, okay?" She paused, and then went on to explain to her mom what had been going on. "When Grace didn't get one of the main roles for the *Grand Défilé*, her mom seemed to think it was because Grace hadn't performed well enough—and she said Grace should stay in school every weekend from now on, to do extra practice. But Mom, I think Grace needs a break."

"I see," her mom said slowly. "I'm inclined to agree with you, honey," she went on. "But don't you think Grace's mom might not like the idea of Grace coming to our place for the weekend? If she's specifically said that Grace should stay in school, then . . ."

Ellie's shoulders slumped as she realized that her mom was right. She hadn't really considered the fact that Grace's mom might well say no. And, now that she thought of it, Ellie realized that Grace herself was going to need a whole lot of persuading if she was to leave the ballet studio behind for a whole weekend.

"Speak to Grace anyway," her mom went on. "If she wants to come to Oxford, then I can try to get her mother to agree, too."

"Thanks, Mom," Ellie replied. "You're the best!"

Humming cheerfully, she went back up toward the dorm. The more she thought about it, the more she thought Grace coming to Oxford with her for the weekend was a stroke of genius. *We can hang out with Bethany and Phoebe*, she thought happily, *and all talk of ballet and end-of-year performances will be BANNED!*

But first, she had to persuade both Grace and her mom that it was a good idea, too, of course. Still, nothing ventured . . .

Smiling to herself, Ellie pushed open the dorm door, to see Grace looking flustered and tearful. "Ellie, have *you* seen my English book?" she asked before Ellie had taken another step. "I can't find it anywhere—and I need it for my prep!"

Ellie shook her head. "Where did you leave it?" she asked in surprise. Grace was pretty much the neatest person in the dorm. *She* never had to search for her work under her bed! For Grace to lose one of her own books was almost impossible.

"Right there on my bedside table," Grace replied.

Ellie looked over at where she was pointing and saw a neat stack of schoolbooks. "And it's not there?" she asked, going over and starting to look through them.

"No!" Grace said. "I knew I should have put them away instead of just leaving them there before character class. This is what happens when you don't do everything the way you should, isn't it?"

"Well, it must be here somewhere," Ellie said reasonably. "Books don't just disappear into thin air."

"What's the problem?" Lara asked, strolling into the dorm just then.

"Lara, have you seen my—" Grace stopped as she spotted something in Lara's hand. "Lara! Is that my English book?"

Lara handed it over. "Yes," she replied. "I just borrowed it to copy up the notes I missed from this afternoon. It was right there on your table, and you weren't around to ask, so—"

"I was practicing downstairs," Grace interrupted. She clutched the book possessively. "You shouldn't just take things that don't belong to you!"

Lara looked taken aback. "Sorry, Grace," she said. "I didn't think you'd mind."

"Well, I do. Don't do it again!" Grace snapped.

Lara shot Grace an offended look. "All right, all right," she muttered, walking off to her bed and throwing a couple of books messily down onto it. "No need to yell at me."

Grace had tears in her eyes, and Ellie put her arm around her. "Come on, Grace," she said. "Lara didn't mean any harm."

"I know, but . . ." Grace sighed. "You can't just go around helping yourself to other people's things!"

Ellie passed Grace a tissue. "Here," she said. "Actually, I was just coming to ask you something," she went on, changing the subject quickly. "How would you like to come back to Oxford with me this weekend? I've asked my mom and she says it's all fine so . . ."

Grace was shaking her head already. "I don't think my mum will let me," she said in a quiet voice. "And anyway, I need to practice."

"You know, you *don't* need to practice every single weekend," Ellie reasoned. "Although if you're really desperate to, there's a

barre all set up in my bedroom back home. You could use that."
There was a pause while Grace digested this, and Ellie plowed on,
not wanting Grace to interrupt with any further objections. "I'm
sure my mom can convince your mom that it's a good idea," she
added. "And hey, we could meet up with Bethany, couldn't we? It
must be a long time since you last saw her."

Grace was silent for a few moments. "I *would* like to see
Bethany again," she said eventually. "I was always disappointed
she didn't get into The Royal Ballet School with us."

Bethany was Ellie's friend from Oxford who'd been at the same
JA class in London with Ellie, Grace, and Matt. She was a really
good dancer who'd just missed out on a place at Lower School.

"Well, fingers crossed your mom thinks it's a good idea, then,"
Ellie said. "Right?"

Grace hesitated for a moment, clearly battling with her
feelings.

"Come on, say yes," Ellie urged. "Aren't you just dying to get
out of school for a day or so?"

Something in Grace's face seemed to give at Ellie's
words, and then she nodded. "Okay," she said with just a glimmer
of a smile.

"Great," Ellie said, smiling back and dialing her home number
at once. "Then I'll get my mom to call your mom right away," she
said. "And with my mom's powers of persuasion, it's almost a done
deal already!"

Dear Diary,

I'm really hoping Grace's mom will agree to Grace coming to Oxford with me. Grace is starting to come around to the idea, too, and keeps talking about Bethany and remembering funny things she used to do at JAs. Go, Mom!

One thing's for sure: Grace seriously needs a break. The way she flipped about Lara borrowing her book was way over the top. And she's gone off to the studio to practice AGAIN now. She was up early this morning to get in extra practice then, too. What can I say to her, though? It's impossible to stop her. I tried to persuade her into doing some prep together tonight, but she didn't want to and started being all defensive again.

Oh, I so hope she can have a weekend in Oxford with me. PLEASE let Mom manage to persuade Grace's mom that it's a good idea!

Chapter 7

"She's here!" Ellie cried, waving out of the dorm window. "Grace, have you got everything?"

It was Saturday morning, and Ellie's mom's car was pulling into the White Lodge driveway. Grace's mom had agreed to the weekend visit—with a little persuasion from Mrs. Brown. And now that she had gotten used to the idea, Grace actually seemed to be happy about the break herself. She had spent a long time the previous evening writing a list of clothes she needed and folding everything carefully into her weekend bag.

At the news that Ellie's mom was here, though, Grace suddenly unzipped her bag and started pulling everything out again.

"Grace?" Ellie said in surprise. "What are you doing? We've got to go—Mom's down there waiting for us."

"I know, but I just . . ." Grace's voice was a little muffled as she bent over her bag looking through it. "I just need to check everything's in there. Socks, knickers, jeans, skirt, shorts . . ."

Ellie stood there with her own weekend bag over her shoulder. "Listen, don't worry about it," she said breezily. "If you have forgotten something—which I'm sure you haven't because you packed so carefully—but if you have, you can always borrow something of mine. Or we can pick something up in town. Or . . ."

". . . Hairbrush, shampoo, conditioner, comb . . ." Now Grace was looking through her toiletries bag.

Ellie sighed, starting to feel impatient. This was precious weekend time that Grace was wasting!

"Okay, I've got everything," Grace finally said, putting her things carefully back into the bag. "I'm ready!"

•   •   •   •

However much she enjoyed being at The Royal Ballet School, it was always great to come back to Oxford, Ellie thought happily as they stepped into the large, sunny apartment that was home. "Let's just dump our bags in my room," she told Grace, "and then we can walk along the river into town, if you want. You haven't been to Oxford before, have you? It is so gorgeous."

Grace unzipped her bag and started taking out her clothes. "I'll just figure out my things first," she said. "Is there a drawer or wardrobe I could use, Ellie?"

"Um . . . sure," Ellie said, opening one of her own drawers and scooping out an armful of T-shirts and tank tops. "Is this okay?"

"Yes, perfect," Grace replied. "Thanks." She began to carefully lay each item of her clothing into the drawer, smoothing down each one as she went.

Ellie watched her uneasily. She'd been hoping that Grace

might stop all this finicky behavior, being out of school. But clearly it wasn't going to be that easy.

"I thought we'd eat out tonight, girls," said Ellie's mom, sticking her head around the bedroom door. "I've booked us a table at a nice new Italian restaurant that recently opened up around the corner. And I've invited Phoebe and Bethany to come along, too," she added with a smile. "We'll pick Pheebs up on the way, of course." Phoebe lived just across the hall. "And Bethany's dad has offered to run her across town to the restaurant and pick her up again."

"Oh, awesome, thanks, Mom!" Ellie said, beaming back at her. "You've thought of everything."

"I'll have to iron this skirt before we go out later," Grace said thoughtfully. She held up a pretty pink skirt and frowned at it. "Look—it has at least three creases in it. And which top should I wear? I'm bound to have to iron that, too," she added, the now-familiar anxious expression returning to her face.

Ellie looked questioningly at her mom, not quite sure what to say in response to Grace.

"It's a very casual kind of place," Ellie's mom assured Grace. "Really, you'll be fine going in what you're wearing now if you want to."

Grace nodded. But her eyes were still scanning her clothes worriedly.

Ellie grabbed Grace's hand. "Come on, Grace—you can decide

later. Let's go for that walk into town."

•   •   •   •

As they walked along the river together, Grace seemed to relax a little. It was a warm, sunny afternoon and peaceful, save for the quacking of ducks and the laughter of people who were gliding slowly along the river in punts—strange flat-bottomed boats that were propelled forward by long poles that the punters pushed into the bottom of the riverbed. There was something very soothing about being by the riverside, Ellie thought contentedly, watching the water swirl by them.

Once in town, the girls treated themselves to an ice cream and sat in the lush green Christ Church Meadow to eat it, enjoying the warmth of the sun on their faces.

"This is the life," Ellie said, kicking her sandals off and wriggling her bare toes in the grass.

"It is," Grace agreed. "Thanks for asking me, Ellie. This is heavenly!" She finished her ice cream and lay down in the grass.

Ellie watched a group of students playing around at the water's edge for a few moments, and then turned to say something to Grace—only to close her mouth again when she realized her friend had fallen fast asleep. Ellie studied her friend's pale face. Her mouth was relaxed, her forehead crease-free—slackened from the intense, anxious expression Ellie had become used to seeing lately.

Ellie put her hands behind her head and closed her eyes, too.

I won't wake her, she thought. *Hey, I might even do the same. This is supposed to be a relaxing weekend, isn't it?*

•   •   •   •

After a lazy afternoon drowsing in the meadow, the girls returned back to the apartment to get dressed for the evening. Grace had changed her mind three times about what she was going to wear and had ironed and ironed! And then she'd spent forever brushing her hair so that it would fall just so.

Before they knew it, Steve, Ellie's stepdad, was knocking on the bedroom door asking them to get a move on, because they were going to be late for their table.

"Grace, you look great," Ellie said, slipping her feet into her sandals. "Come on!"

"Are you sure?" Grace asked doubtfully, staring at herself in the mirror. Then she shook her head. "I don't," she said glumly. "What a mess. What a mess I look!" She picked up her hairbrush again and began brushing her hair frenziedly.

Ellie was shocked to see that Grace's hands were trembling, the knuckles white, as they gripped the brush and yanked it through her hair.

"Hey! Easy!" Ellie cried in alarm. She put a hand on Grace's to slow the brushing. "Shall I do it for you?" she asked. "You're going to pull it all out by the roots like that."

Ellie's tone was light, but she was starting to feel anxious herself. Grace was going to hurt herself at this rate.

Thankfully, Grace let Ellie take over. As Ellie gently gathered up her friend's hair to tie it into a ponytail, she saw that Grace's scalp now looked decidedly pink and sore. This wasn't right, was it? This couldn't be right.

"There," Ellie said. "Now come on, before Steve has to hurry us along again. Let's go and get Phoebe."

Phoebe answered the door in jeans and a plain pink T-shirt. "Hi, Ellie! Hi, Grace!" she cried, giving them both hugs. "Gosh, Grace, you look very smart," she added. "I feel a bit scruffy next to you."

Grace's eyes widened and she plucked at her skirt. "Do you think it's too much? Am I overdressed?" she asked anxiously.

"Oh, no, Grace—I didn't mean that!" Phoebe replied hurriedly.

"You look great, Grace," Ellie said, shepherding Grace along the hallway. "Let's go—otherwise Bethany will be waiting for us at the restaurant all on her own."

"Honestly, you girls," Steve said good-naturedly as they walked along to the restaurant. "I've been ready for ages!"

Ellie's mom turned to roll her eyes and grin at them. "Don't pay attention to him, girls," she said. "He only got back from playing football twenty minutes ago. And I had to iron his shirt for him so we wouldn't be late."

Just as they arrived outside the restaurant, Ellie saw Bethany being dropped off by her dad across the street. "Hi!" she called excitedly.

Bethany turned and waved manically, then kissed her dad and came bounding over to them.

The three girls all greeted Bethany, while Ellie's mom and Bethany's dad figured out what time he should come and pick her up later.

Then they all waved him off and went inside.

This was such a great idea, Ellie told herself happily, as they were shown to their table. *This is exactly what Grace needed—an afternoon nap, and now a fun evening with friends. Dr. Ellie to the rescue!*

"It's so great to see you again, Grace," Bethany said in her usual chatty way. "And I can't wait to see you dancing! Did Ellie's mom tell you, she's gotten us tickets to come and see you two in the Saturday matinee performance at The Royal Opera House? I can't wait!"

"Me neither!" Phoebe chimed in with a smile.

"I cannot wait to see the *Grand Défilé*," Bethany went on excitedly. "Mrs. Franklin says it's always wonderful. Have you started rehearsing for it yet?" Even though she didn't get into The Royal Ballet School, Bethany still loved ballet, and continued to take classes at the Franklin Dance Academy in Oxford, where Ellie had first met her.

Grace's smile seemed to freeze on her face. "Yes," she said guardedly. Her glance flicked over at Ellie.

"And we all know Grace is going to be fantastic," Ellie said quickly. "Oh, look, here come the menus!" she said in relief. "What does everybody want to eat?"

As everyone started oohing and aahing at the delicious-sounding dishes on the menu, Ellie cast a look at Grace. Her friend wasn't looking at the menu at all. She was repositioning her silverware again and again—like she had begun to do with the things on her bedside shelf in the dorm.

"Garlic bread!" Phoebe said, her eyes lighting up as she read through the starters. "Ooh, but they've got garlic mushrooms, too! No . . . wait! Stuffed peppers! What an impossible decision!" The others laughed.

And then, to Ellie's relief, Grace left her silverware alone for two minutes and picked up her menu. "It all sounds gorgeous," she said, a smile appearing on her face at last.

•   •   •   •

Grace stayed rather quiet throughout the starters, letting the others make most of the conversation. She got excited when the topic turned to a pop group that she liked, but then, as soon as Bethany mentioned ballet again, she seemed to withdraw into herself.

The main courses arrived, and as she forked up a mouthful of her spaghetti bolognese, a tiny drop of pasta sauce splashed onto one of her sleeves. "Oh, no!" she gasped in dismay. She grabbed up her napkin and began to dab frantically at the small stain.

A passing waitress saw what had happened. "I'll get you a

cloth," she said kindly.

"Don't worry. I have a wet wipe right here in my bag—that'll do the trick," said Ellie's mom, pulling it out. "Here, Grace—let's get that stain out for you." She dabbed away at Grace's sleeve until the spot of sauce had vanished. "There," she said with a smile. "All better."

With the sauce wiped clean, the conversation turned to everybody's food.

"This is just delicious," said Bethany happily. She took another huge bite of her seafood pizza. "How's your tagliatelle, Pheebs?"

Phoebe wound some of her pasta around her fork and held it up. "Mmmm," she sighed, licking her lips. "Mamma mia!"

Ellie saw that Grace wasn't eating. She was still examining her sleeve and rubbing at it, even though the wet wipe had made it perfectly clean. "How's your spaghetti, Grace?" Ellie prompted.

"Sorry?" Grace asked, tearing her eyes away from her sleeve.

"Your pasta," Ellie said, pointing to her plate. "Is it okay?" she asked, willing Grace to act normally and forget all about her sleeve.

"Oh, yes," Grace said, picking up her fork again. "Lovely, thanks." She began eating mechanically, but her eyes kept going back to her sleeve. It was as though she could still feel the stain there, even though it wasn't visible.

Ellie caught Bethany staring quizzically at Grace and sighed.

It wasn't too surprising, really, but the last time Bethany had seen Grace, Grace hadn't yet developed any of her strange habits and behaviors. The difference in Grace must be really obvious to Bethany, Ellie realized.

It was almost like Grace was becoming totally fixated on trying to be perfect the whole time, Ellie thought. She gazed unhappily at her friend. What could she say about it to Grace, though? Grace was so sensitive, she'd think Ellie was criticizing her and she'd get all defensive. And that would be no help at all.

Ellie excused herself and went to the bathroom. Bethany caught Ellie's eye and excused herself, too.

As soon as they were out of earshot, Bethany turned to Ellie. "What's up with Grace?" she asked bluntly. "She's being weird. She goes all quiet every time we talk about ballet—and she seems obsessed with that tiny little mark on her sleeve—which isn't even there anymore!"

Ellie shrugged helplessly. "I know that she's stressed about the end-of-year performances—she always does get stressed about performing. And her mom seems to be putting more pressure on her than ever," Ellie explained with a sigh. "As far as I know, there's nothing else. But you're right. She's definitely acting strangely. And I don't know what to do."

"I think you should tell somebody at school," Bethany advised as they went into the bathroom. "Because if you ask me, she needs help."

Dear Diary,

　I'm really worried now about all the weird habits Grace has taken up lately. Maybe there really is something seriously wrong with her. I guess I've been living with her, so the oddness has kind of crept up on me. But tonight, Bethany—who was last with Grace when she was completely okay—saw the changes in her all at once. And she said that she thinks Grace needs help.

　I think she's right—Grace's strange behavior is definitely getting worse, not better. But what should I do? I need help, to help Grace!

　Maybe Jessica might know what to do. I'll go and talk to her when we get back to school. I really hope she can help me—because I'm feeling pretty stuck right now.

・　　・　　・　　・

Back at school on Sunday night, Ellie went to find Jessica, her Year 8 guide, to ask her advice. She found her alone in the computer room writing e-mails.

"Hi, Ellie," Jessica smiled up at her. "Everything okay?"

Ellie sat down at the terminal next to Jessica. "Not really, Jessica," Ellie replied quietly. "I'm hoping you might be able to help . . ."

Jessica immediately turned away from her terminal to give Ellie her full attention. "I will if I can," she said seriously. "What's up?"

"Well, a friend of mine has been acting kind of strangely . . ." Ellie began hesitantly. She began telling Jessica about all of the weird things Grace had been doing lately.

Jessica listened to Ellie's concerns, her face serious. "Ellie," she began gently, "this friend of yours . . . you can tell me, you know—are you talking about yourself?"

Ellie shook her head. "No," she said. "No, honestly, it's not me," she said. She felt her cheeks grow hot with Jessica's gaze upon her. "It's a friend. I can't tell you who, though."

Jessica smiled. "Okay, sorry," she said. "I had to ask, though. Anyway, I've heard about things like this happening to other students—though it's rare. And I suppose it might get worse in the summer term and become really noticeable when there's exam pressure as well as the end-of-year performances to prepare for," she went on. "People react to too much pressure in different ways: Some just get bad-tempered or tearful. Others develop eating problems—eating too much or too little. We talked about that in a class we had on nutrition. And then there's OCD . . ."

"What's that?" Ellie asked blankly.

"Obsessive-compulsive disorder," Jessica told her. "It sounds to me as though your friend might have it. My sister's best friend, Stacey, had OCD. That's how I know about it. Her thing was washing her hands all the time—constantly, until they were red, raw, and sore. Hang on, let me bring up something on the Net for you to see." Jessica typed "obsessive-compulsive disorder" into a search engine, and then brought up a website.

Ellie scanned through the symptoms listed on the computer screen in front of her.

- Compulsive checking and rechecking . . .
- Repetitive rituals . . .
- Obsessive need for order and symmetry— a desire to align objects "just so" . . .
- Fixations upon cleanliness or tidiness or hygiene
- Abnormal concerns about the neatness of one's personal appearance . . .

Ellie nodded slowly as she read. "That sounds kind of like a checklist for what Grace—I mean, my friend—is doing," she said. Her cheeks flamed. She hadn't meant to mention Grace's name, but it had just slipped out.

Jessica gave Ellie a reassuring hug. "Don't worry. I won't tell anyone that it's Grace," she assured Ellie. "Cross my heart, I won't." She thought for a moment. "But if you've seen these symptoms in her, then I think she does need help. And the sooner the better."

Ellie sighed. She'd known in her heart that Grace would need help. "But will she be all right again?" she asked. "Once she gets help, I mean."

Jessica nodded. "I should think so. Stacey's fine now," she said. "She went to see a specialist and had counseling, and now the hand-washing has stopped. But it's one of those things that can get really out of control if it isn't confronted."

Ellie nodded. That made sense. Already she'd seen Grace's odd habits become more frequent. "Maybe I should have done something earlier," she said, feeling wretched. "But at first, I thought she was just being a bit fussy. And then, over the weekend, a friend who hadn't seen Grace for ages spotted right away that she was different, and . . ."

Jessica patted her arm reassuringly. "Hey, don't be hard on yourself," she said. "It's often people closest to OCD sufferers who are the last to realize it—because the obsessions build up gradually."

"I guess," Ellie replied slowly. "So . . . should I confront her with it, do you think?" she asked.

"In a gentle kind of way, I think so," Jessica agreed. "Do you want me to come with you, to talk to her?"

Ellie shook her head. "I don't think she'd want anyone else to know about it," she said. "Thanks—but I'll talk to her myself first, and try to persuade her to talk to Mrs. Hall about it."

"Okay," Jessica said. "But if there's anything else I can do, then just tell me."

"Thanks, Jessica," Ellie replied gratefully. "I will." She heaved a sigh. "Which just leaves me to go and ask Grace about what's going on in her head. I guess I'd better go and get it over with."

"Good luck," Jessica said. "You're doing the right thing, Ellie."

•   •   •   •

It didn't *feel* like the right thing anymore to Ellie, a few minutes later.

She'd found Grace practicing in one of the studios, her cheeks red with exertion and her hair damp with sweat. *I guess I just have to bite the bullet*, she thought grimly. "Grace . . . may I talk to you a moment?" she asked, shutting the studio door behind her as she went in.

Grace finished the steps she'd been practicing and came over.

"I was just wondering . . . is everything okay?" Ellie blurted out. "It's just that . . . You seem kind of stressed-out. You're working really hard and . . ."

"I'm fine," Grace said at once, raising her knee and kicking out her toes. "Absolutely fine."

"It's just . . . well . . ." Ellie faltered. *How* did you go about telling your best friend that you thought they needed help to sort out their strange behavior?

"Absolutely fine," Grace said, moving back to the barre. "Now, I must get this step right, so . . ."

"No!" Ellie said hurriedly. "No, I don't think you are fine, Grace!" The blood rushed into her cheeks as she saw the defensive light in Grace's eyes. *Oh Grace, I don't want to hurt your feelings but . . .* Ellie took a deep breath. "You've been getting so uptight about little things recently, Grace," she went on. "Like Lara borrowing your book . . . and having a loose hair in your bun or a crease in your skirt—and what about when there was that tiny speck of blood on your duvet cover and you totally freaked about it? And how upset you got at the mark on your sleeve in the restaurant—when it wasn't even there anymore! And—"

Ellie stopped, her heart thumping. Grace's eyes were bright— she looked as if she was about to cry! Ellie wondered for an awful second if she'd gone too far. "Grace, I'm not trying to give you a hard time," she continued, as gently as she could. "Just the opposite—I want to help you." It was time for the difficult part. "I might be wrong, but I've heard about something called OCD. Obsessive-compulsive disorder? And I think . . ." She met Grace's gaze. "I think you might have it."

There was a long, heavy silence.

"And why do you think that?" Grace asked eventually, her voice cool and defensive.

Ellie wished and wished they weren't having this conversation. *You're doing the right thing, Ellie,* she heard Jessica say in her head, and plowed on. "I read some stuff on the Internet," she said. "About how, when you have OCD, it's like you feel you're not in control over big things in your life, so you become really obsessed with the smaller things that you feel you *can* control. You know how you've been checking your ballet things before classes? And the way you checked everything all over again before we went to my mom's? And how upset you've been getting when your hair or clothes aren't totally how you think they should be?"

There was another awful silence.

Ellie started to feel horrible inside. Grace was looking as if Ellie had just slapped her or something.

"I can't believe you're saying all this to me, Ellie. I thought we were supposed to be *friends*!" Grace said heatedly, and then she stormed out of the studio.

Ellie felt like crying. *Oh, no!* How could things have gone so wrong? The way Grace had just glared at her as she stomped off, it was as if she hated her. Ellie put her head in her hands. What now? Where did she go from here? She just wanted to help Grace. . . .

She sighed. The first thing she had to do was find Grace and apologize for upsetting her.

But just as she reached the studio door, it swung open. And there was Grace again, with a strange look on her face.

"Ellie, I think—" she started to say, but then she seemed to choke on her words. Her face crumpled and tears began streaming down her cheeks.

"Oh, Grace," Ellie said, feeling tears spring to her own eyes. She rushed to put her arms around her friend. "Oh, Grace, I'm sorry I had to say all those things. But I know that something's wrong and I can't just pretend it isn't."

Grace buried her head in her hands and sobbed. "It's like . . . I just feel like I have to be the best all the time!" she cried. "And in ballet, I always was—until I came here. And my mum—she just won't have it that sometimes, I'm just not . . ." Her words were lost in a fresh torrent of weeping.

Ellie hugged her friend, feeling wretched for her. "I know," she said.

"My mum has always wanted me to be a ballerina," Grace went on, still crying. "She was a dancer herself, but never got a place at The Royal Ballet School, never made her own dream come true."

"Which is why she pushes you so hard," Ellie guessed aloud.

Grace nodded as fresh tears streamed down her cheeks. "And I don't want to let her down," she confessed. "I just want her to be proud of me."

"Of course she's proud of you!" Ellie said at once. "Who wouldn't be, Grace? You're amazing—you're so talented! You beat off hundreds and hundreds of other girls to get a place here at The Royal Ballet School and you're one of the best dancers in our year. I mean—who wouldn't be proud of that?"

Grace said nothing, but she had stopped crying at least. Then she said in a shaky-sounding voice, "I think you might be right. About the OCD." She bit her lip and turned to Ellie, tears still glistening in her eyes. "But I don't think I can stop it," she added in a whisper.

Ellie squeezed Grace's hand. "I'll help you, Grace," she said, hoping with all her heart that she'd be able to.

Dear Diary,

What a night! It all started happening with Grace. She agreed to tell Mrs. Hall about her problem. We went together, and Mrs. Hall was really great about it. Poor Grace burst into tears all over again, though. Mrs. Hall hugged her and said that it could all be worked out. Grace shouldn't think that she was sick or a freak—she was just under too much pressure.

Mrs. Hall said that she'd talk to the school nurse about it, and then either she or the nurse would talk to Grace's mom and ask for permission to refer Grace to a specialist counselor. So things are starting to happen now and hopefully this is the start of Grace being happy again. I hope so.

I'm just so relieved that she's acknowledged the problem—for a while, I thought she was just going to freeze me out and get really mad at me for talking about it with her.

It's so hard to see my best friend so upset, and not be able to do anything to help. But now, I hope she'll get to talk to someone who can.

Chapter 8

Mrs. Hall was as good as her word. On Monday after lunch, she asked Grace into her office for a quick chat.

Grace immediately grabbed Ellie's hand and pulled her along, too. "Will you come with me? Please?" she begged.

"Sure," Ellie agreed.

With a smile, Mrs. Hall gestured for the two girls to take a seat. Then she closed the door and sat down herself. "I just wanted to let you know that I called your mum this morning, Grace, to tell her how things are," she said.

Grace looked stricken. "Oh! What did she say? Is she really angry with me?" she asked urgently.

Mrs. Hall shook her head. "No, Grace," she replied gently. "She isn't angry with you. She's worried, obviously, and said she hadn't realized you felt under so much strain. But no, she isn't angry at all."

"Okay," Grace said. But she still looked anxious—as if she didn't really believe it.

"She's going to call you later on to talk about it with you," Mrs. Hall went on. "When I spoke with her, I didn't spell out that most of the pressure you've been feeling has been coming from her. I thought that was probably something you two should talk about together, when you feel ready."

"But she'll be so upset!" Grace said desperately.

Ellie leaned over and took Grace's hand. "But Grace, it's making you upset in the meantime, and your mom wouldn't want that either," she pointed out gently.

Grace bit her lip, mulling it over. "I guess," she said.

"Your mum said that she'd come to your counseling sessions with you, if you want," Mrs. Hall went on. "Although I imagine you might not want her there at first. It's for you to decide, anyway. The nurse is trying to fix something up for this week."

"So soon?" Grace asked, looking shocked. "I'm not sure I'm ready to talk about it all with a stranger yet. And I definitely don't want Mum there, listening, while I talk about her."

Mrs. Hall patted Grace's hand. "Listen, if you'd like to talk to your mum now instead of waiting until she calls you later, you're very welcome to use my phone," she suggested.

Grace thought for a moment, and then nodded. "Yes, please," she said. "I'll get it over with." She gave Ellie a watery smile. "I'll see you in geography. Would you mind telling Mr. Whitehouse I'm going to be late?"

"Sure," Ellie said, getting to her feet. "Good luck, Grace."

•   •   •   •

When Grace appeared in the geography class half an hour or

so later, her eyes were a little red and her cheeks were blotchy, but she was smiling. Surely that was a good sign?

"Mum was really shocked about it all—but nice," she whispered to Ellie as she sat down. "We had a long talk about everything. It was really difficult to get the words right, but I told her about the pressure she makes me feel to be the best dancer in The Royal Ballet School—and how anything less made me feel a total failure—and how I just can't cope with that anymore."

"Well done, Grace," Ellie said. "That took guts. What did she say to that?"

Grace rubbed her eyes. "She said she was really sorry that she hadn't noticed she'd been pushing me too hard," she told Ellie. "And she started saying what a rubbish mum she must be and how awful she felt about it, and she cried, and then I cried, too. But by the time we said good-bye, everything was all right." Her breath came out of her in a long exhalation. "I feel so much better!" she finished.

"Phew!" Ellie replied, feeling massive relief for her friend that it was all now out in the open. "I'm really glad you told her how you felt."

Mr. Whitehouse clapped his hands for attention. "If you remember, I asked you to learn a list of Ordnance Survey symbols," he said. "Let's see who managed it. Kate, we'll start with you." Mr. Whitehouse began chalking up symbols on the board. "Can you tell me what this one means?"

Kate looked blankly at the pink triangle Mr. Whitehouse was pointing to. "Um . . . a mountain?" she guessed.

Mr. Whitehouse shook his head, his eyebrows coming together in a long-suffering frown. "Kate, I didn't even give you a 'mountain' symbol to learn," he said. "Did you even *look* through the list?"

"Um . . . yes," Kate faltered, turning bright red.

"I hope so," Mr. Whitehouse told her, his blue eyes fixed all the while upon her face. "Because the exams are coming up soon, and this is all stuff you have to know, guys. And you really *should* know it by now!" He addressed the room. "So, who can tell me what this symbol *does* mean?"

Toby put his hand up. "A youth hostel, sir," he said.

Mr. Whitehouse nodded. "Good. Who's next?" His eyes roved the room. "Matt. Can you tell me what this symbol is used for?"

Mr. Whitehouse pointed to the next symbol along, a square with a small cross on top, and Matt nodded. "A church," he replied.

"A church with a . . . ?" Mr. Whitehouse prompted.

Matt looked uncharacteristically ruffled. "Um . . . a tower?" he replied hesitantly.

"Good guess, Matt," said Mr. Whitehouse with a grin. "Correct."

Matt grinned back, but Ellie noticed that his ears had gone red. They always did when he was embarrassed.

"Sophie," said Mr. Whitehouse, "you next. What's this one?"

As they went through the list of symbols, it became clear that the class's knowledge of them was somewhat sketchy.

Ellie herself hadn't had much time to spend memorizing them, what with going away all weekend, and then talking to Jessica, Grace, and Mrs. Hall last night. Luckily the symbol she was tested on was one she knew—marshland—and she escaped the wrath of her teacher, but others weren't so lucky.

At the end of class, Mr. Whitehouse addressed them in an unusually serious tone. "Year 7, I know you all want to be ballet dancers," he began, "but your academic work is taken very seriously here, too, you know. You've got exams soon and you won't be able to wing them. You have to put the hours in—just as you do with your dancing." He held up a stack of papers. "So for prep tonight, I'm going to set you the same list of symbols to learn all over again, and I've got another twenty here for you to learn, too."

A groan went around the room, but Mr. Whitehouse ignored it. "There'll be a written test on the symbols next Wednesday," he finished, as the end-of-lesson bell rang.

Ellie sighed as she and Grace gathered up their books and pens to move on to their next class. Work, work, and more work. She'd been right about this being a tough half-term—and by the sound of things, it was set to get way tougher still!

•   •   •   •

"Does my hair look okay?" Grace asked fretfully. "Only it looks wispy to me. What do you think?"

Ellie looked at her friend. "Guess what I'm going to say," she said quietly.

Grace turned bright red, and Ellie, not wanting to make her friend feel bad, went over and gave her a hug. Grace's body felt tense but then she seemed to loosen up and relax.

"You're going to say it looks fine," Grace said sheepishly.

"Absolutely fine," Ellie said firmly. "Really and truly fine, so try not to worry about it, Grace."

The two girls were in the dorm the following day, getting changed after ballet, along with the other girls. The only difference was that while Ellie and the others were going on to their IT class, Grace was due to start her first counseling session instead.

Grace had opted to have her first couple of sessions alone with the counselor. She wanted to talk about her relationship with her mom without her mom being there. The plan was that Mrs. Tennant would then accompany Grace a couple of sessions later, on the following Monday.

"Hopefully by then, I'll feel ready to talk about it all with her face-to-face," Grace had confided in Ellie. "But now that it's about to happen, I'm scared," Grace suddenly said, putting down her hairbrush. "Ellie, I'm not sure I want to do this. I think I've changed my mind."

Ellie took Grace's hands. "You'll be fine," she said. "And you're getting out of IT, you lucky girl. I just know Mrs. Sanderson is going to be on the warpath about how late I handed in my prep."

Lara looked across curiously. "Everything okay, Grace?" she asked.

Grace nodded vigorously and busied herself buttoning up her blouse. "I've got a dentist appointment, that's all," she said, not looking at Lara or Ellie. "Just a little nervous in case I need a filling."

Ellie said nothing about Grace's lie. If it had been her, she would want to keep her counseling appointment private, too.

"Well, good luck, anyway," Ellie said, picking up her IT folder. "See you at lunchtime."

• • • •

It was difficult for Ellie to find a private minute with Grace to discuss the counseling session that afternoon. At lunchtime, the canteen was always so busy and noisy that it was almost impossible to talk confidentially to somebody—and today was no exception. Then afterward, even though Ellie and Grace slipped out of the canteen together, Sophie and Lara caught up with them and joined them to sit outside in the garden. After that, they were into their afternoon classes—history, music, and chemistry—without so much as a minute on their own.

Ellie had managed a quick "You okay?" and Grace had nodded, but that had been the only conversation they'd had about it. It was hardly the light type of gossip that could be talked about over the lab table in chemistry, either. Ellie *had* noticed that Grace seemed rather quiet since she'd returned from the counseling session, though.

At last, chemistry was over. Ellie and Grace both cleaned up the bench they'd shared in the chemistry lab extra slowly, and then, after everyone had gone off to tuck, Ellie was finally able to ask.

"So how was it?"

Grace's expression was thoughtful. "The counselor was really nice," she said, "but the situation felt a little weird, to be honest." She lowered her voice. "It was all really unnatural—hey, let's talk to this complete stranger about the most personal things going on in your mind. Like it's that easy."

"I can imagine," Ellie said sympathetically. "It must have been hard to know where to start—and exactly what to say."

"Yes, and I felt funny about telling her private stuff at first," Grace went on. "Some things I didn't want to speak about at all in case she thought I was bonkers . . ."

"Oh, Grace!" Ellie said. "Of course she wouldn't think that!"

"But when I finally *did* start telling her—Maura, she's called—about, you know . . . what's been happening . . . she was really supportive," Grace went on. "She doesn't think I have OCD, but something like it, called OCPD, that's easier to treat. She's made me think about stuff that I've never really thought about before—mostly to do with my mum. About how all this time I've been trying to please her. And she told me that I need to start thinking seriously about me. What I want, for a change."

"Good," Ellie said firmly. "That's how it should be."

As they made their way to the canteen, Grace smiled suddenly. "And what I want right now," she declared, "is a cup of tea and some cake."

Ellie grinned. "You go, girl—follow your heart," she joked. "Maura would be proud of you."

●　　　●　　　●　　　●

Grace had another counseling session on Thursday, and came out of that session even more pensive than she'd been before. She seemed lost in her own world, and Ellie was dismayed to see her go off for extra ballet practice again that evening—and again on Friday evening. She'd been hoping that Grace's counseling was going to stop her friend from pushing herself to the limit all the time—but clearly that wasn't going to happen just yet.

I guess the counseling can't change things overnight, Ellie tried to reassure herself, as she turned back to her prep.

After ballet class on Saturday morning, there was a school trip to Kew Gardens. Ellie was expecting to have to spend forever persuading Grace to leave the ballet studio behind to come along— but to her surprise, Grace decided all on her own that she would have a day off from her extra practicing and go on the trip. Ellie was delighted. This was progress!

It was another gorgeous sunny day—perfect for relaxing in a beautiful, tranquil garden. Lara had decided not to come;

she was suffering from hay fever and decided that being outside would make it even worse. Sophie, Kate, Bryony, and Isabelle had decided that they'd rather go on the afternoon trip to Sheen, so there was just Ellie and Grace from their little group of friends going to Kew. Even better.

"Please do try to visit the Palm House when we get to Kew," Mrs. Hall said on the minibus, "as it's probably Kew's best-known glasshouse. It was built between 1844 and 1848 and is the world's most important surviving Victorian glass-and-iron structure." She smiled a little self-consciously. "Well, so my guidebook says, anyway. Definitely worth a look!"

Kew Gardens certainly was a stunning place to be. Walking into the huge, steamy greenhouses—*glasshouses*, Ellie thought, using the correct British term—was like entering a secret rain forest full of exotic, colorful plants that practically dripped with condensation. Ellie was almost expecting to see orangutans dangling from the trees, and bright-feathered parrots squawking. It was hard to believe they were still just outside London, instead of South America.

Outside the greenhouses, tree-lined paths stretched around the grounds and the flower beds were riotous mosaics of color and form. It was like being in an oasis of calm after the hectic few weeks they'd had at school.

"My mom would love this," Ellie said, as they strolled past the lake. "She'd want to stop and look at every single flower."

"Mine too," Grace agreed. She paused. "Whereas I really want to find a shady spot to have a lemonade and watch the world go by. . . ."

Ellie giggled. "You read my mind," she said.

The girls sat down on a patch of grass and sipped their drinks in contented silence for a few minutes.

"This feels good," Ellie said, finishing her juice. "This feels like a real break, doesn't it?"

Grace nodded. "Totally," she sighed happily. "You know, I thought I would feel anxious being here, instead of practicing, but it's okay."

"Good," Ellie said, wondering if Grace was leading the conversation someplace.

"Because talking to Maura has made me realize that I've been totally overdoing the ballet—and for what?" Grace went on. She finished her drink, looking thoughtful again. "Last night and Thursday night, I asked myself: I did all that extra practice and asked myself afterward, did I actually enjoy that? Did it make me happy?" She looked across at Ellie, her eyes troubled. "And do you know what? The first thing I thought was, no, actually. No, I didn't enjoy that. No, I'd much rather have been hanging out in the dorm catching up on letter-writing or doing my prep or watching TV with everyone else."

Ellie wasn't sure what to say. "Well, I never thought you needed extra practice anyway, Grace," she said after a few moments. "But . . ."

"It's been really hard working through some of the questions Maura's been asking me," Grace went on. "But now I've started being honest with myself, I feel just massive relief."

"Good," Ellie replied. "And your mom's going to come to the next counseling session, isn't she?"

Grace nodded. "Yes," she said, "along with Ms. Bell and Mr. Knott." She grimaced. "It's going to be a pretty full house in there." She began twirling a grass stalk around her fingers. "Actually, I'm dreading it," she confessed. "Because I don't think my mum—or Ms. Bell and Mr. Knott—are going to like what I've got to say."

"What do you mean?" Ellie asked, curious to know what Grace might say to concern the Lower School Ballet Principal and the Head of Lower School.

"I mean . . ." Grace bit her lip. "I mean, I'm starting to wonder whether I'm cut out for a career in ballet."

"What?" Ellie gasped.

"Don't get me wrong—I love dancing," Grace went on hurriedly. "It's the pressure of being in the spotlight that I hate. Sometimes it feels like it's too much, like I just want to run away and have a normal life like most other people our age. And I suppose it all comes back to whether I want to go on putting myself through this—or not."

"Grace," Ellie asked nervously, "what are you saying?"

Grace sighed unhappily. "I'm saying, I'm wondering whether I should leave The Royal Ballet School," she said.

Dear Diary,

Talk about a bombshell. I can't believe what Grace told me this afternoon, just can't believe it. She's thinking of leaving The Royal Ballet School!

Even though I know she's found things difficult lately, I truly hadn't seen this one coming. I can't STAND the thought of her leaving—absolutely can't stand it! It's bad enough losing Sophie at the end of term—but Grace too??? I would miss her so much.

Even if she doesn't believe it herself, everybody else knows that she's so talented. It would be awful for her to stop dancing now. I think it would be a mistake—but then again, I'm not the one who's got to make the decision.

I felt so shocked and upset when she told me what she was thinking that I just wanted to beg her to stay—but I knew that would be unfair of me. So I tried to be really mature instead, and told her that whatever she decided, I would support her and respect her decision, and that it was her life at the end of the day.

If I put aside my own feelings about her wanting to stay, then I just want Grace to be happy again—and if that means ending her ballet career, I guess I have to accept it. I hope she has the strength to go through with telling her mom and the school. I know she's completely dreading her mom's reaction. Anyway, she's sworn me to secrecy because she is still trying to make up her mind.

I feel like crying. I sooo want her to stay!

Chapter

9

On Monday morning, Ellie could see just how nervous Grace was about that afternoon's counseling session. She hardly touched her breakfast, and then, before ballet class began, it was as if she'd gone back to her obsessive ways. She spent ages doing and redoing her hair and fussing about her appearance—convinced that her leotard had a smudge of dirt on it.

Ellie watched helplessly, unsure what she should do. Grace's leotard looked spotless, and her hair was as neat as it always was—and yet she'd unpinned it again and was brushing it fiercely. If she drew attention to Grace's obsessive behavior in any way, it might make her friend feel worse. Still, it was very hard to see Grace getting into such a state, and not say anything about it.

She cringed as Sophie called out, in all innocence, "Hurry up there, Grace—you know, you brush your hair so much nowadays, I'm surprised that it hasn't all fallen out!"

Grace turned red, and, for an awful moment, Ellie thought she was about to cry. Ellie quickly held out her hand. "I'll do your hair, Grace," she offered.

Grace silently passed her the brush.

"I wouldn't listen to that Sophie if I were you, Grace—I think she's just jealous of your beautiful locks," Ellie went on, trying to keep the mood lighthearted. "Isn't that right, Soph?"

Sophie laughed good-naturedly. "I'm just jealous of your patience, Grace," she admitted. "My hair has never looked as perfect as yours—it just gets bunged up in its bun any old how." She patted it with a grin. "As you can probably tell."

After the swiftest bun she'd ever rolled, Ellie took Grace's arm and steered her to the door. "We'd better go," she said, "otherwise, we'll be late."

"But my hair . . ." Grace started fretfully. "It still doesn't look quite . . ."

"Your hair's *fine*, Grace," Ellie told her calmly. "Obviously not as perfect as *Sophie's*, but you'll do," she joked. She held her breath. Would Grace take offense at the joke and rush back to brush out her bun all over again?

There was a pause, and then, to Ellie's great relief, Grace gave a weak smile. "You're right. My hair's fine," she agreed. "It's just me that's not . . ." she added in a low voice.

Ellie hugged her friend tightly, and then gently steered her toward the door. "Come on," she said. "Time to go."

•   •   •   •

Grace had arranged to meet her mom after lunch in the school reception area prior to her counseling session. Ellie waited with her until the lunch hour ended. Then she hugged her again and wished her luck. "Not that you'll need it," she said encouragingly. "I know you're strong enough to do this."

"I don't really feel very strong," Grace admitted. "But I'm kind of glad to be getting this figured out now, and telling my mum exactly how I feel about ballet."

Ellie felt a cold, squeezing feeling in her tummy at Grace's words but tried not to show how awful she felt at the very idea of Grace leaving. "Look, there's your mom," she said instead. "Right on time. Hope it all goes well, Grace. Everybody loves you. Remember that."

Ellie slipped away as Mrs. Tennant came through the main entrance, but she could hear the greeting taking place behind her. "Gracie!" she heard Mrs. Tennant cry out. "Oh, darling, are you all right?"

Not yet, Ellie thought as she walked to her next class, *but hopefully she will be soon.* She realized she was clutching her books so tightly, her knuckles had turned white as she walked along. *Oh, please let Grace be okay again soon!*

•　　　•　　　•　　　•

Grace appeared again at tuck, looking as refreshed as if she'd just had twelve hours of solid sleep. "Hiya! Should we eat our tuck outside? I'm dying to talk to you," she whispered to Ellie as she joined her in the line for tea.

"Sure," Ellie said. She felt pleased to see her friend looking so bright-eyed again, but she couldn't help a stab of fear at what this might mean. *Grace has told her mom she wants to leave the school and her mom said, "Fine," and that's why she's so cheerful,* she thought miserably. *I just know it!*

They went outside and sat down on the lawn.

Ellie turned to Grace expectantly. "Well?" she asked.

"It was great," Grace said at once. All the wound-up tension seemed to have vanished from her body. "Just great. Mum actually *listened* to me while I sat there saying that I wasn't sure if I was cut out to stay at The Royal Ballet School because I've been feeling so stressed out about it all."

"And what did she say afterward?" Ellie asked.

"Well, it's more what she *didn't* say, to be honest," Grace replied. "I mean, she didn't just launch into telling me how it was such a great honor to be at The Royal Ballet School, and that I couldn't possibly turn my back on such a wonderful career, blah, blah, blah—which is what I fully expected, and was dreading her saying."

"Good," Ellie said, biting into a cereal bar. "So . . . what *did* she say?"

"She said—get this—that she totally respected whatever I wanted to do," Grace replied happily. "And that she would support me in whatever I chose."

"Wow," Ellie said, raising her eyebrows. "I wasn't expecting that!"

"Me neither," Grace said. "But then she explained why—she told me that she'd been doing a lot of thinking and talking to other people. And that she'd come to the conclusion that she'd been forcing her own ambitions on me, she said. And I said, yes, that's how it always felt to me, too, and that up until now I'd always gone along with it because I want her to be proud of me. But . . ." She shrugged. "Well, you know. It all became too much."

"So . . ." Ellie said cautiously, hardly daring to voice what she hoped this might mean. "Maybe if your mom isn't on your back the whole time, about being the best at everything . . ." She paused, not wanting to badmouth Grace's mom too much. "I mean . . . if things stop being so pressured for you here, then maybe you might start to enjoy being here more. . . . Don't you think?"

Grace smiled. "That's pretty much what Mr. Knott and Ms. Bell said, too," she replied. "They suggested that I stay on here for another year—to see if I do better without the extra pressure from Mum. They said that if I could get into thinking of ballet and performing as being something for me, rather than something for Mum, I might decide that I want to be a ballerina after all."

Ellie took a deep breath. "So . . . are you going to think about staying?" she asked. She tried to keep her voice light, but she felt very nervous about what Grace would reply.

Grace hesitated—and then nodded. "I'll think about it . . ." she said slowly. "But there's so much other stuff going on right now—the end-of-year exams coming up and then the end-of-year performances, of course—my head's just full to bursting with it all. I'm just going to wait and see how I feel at the end of term. It's too big a decision to rush through."

"You're right," Ellie said. "This is an awful time to have to make such a big choice. I'm sure once we're at the end of term you'll be able to see more clearly. You know, if you feel yourself getting excited about the thought of being in Year 8 . . . or, if you feel like you just can't wait to get out of this place . . ." She gave Grace a big hug. "Anyway, I'm really proud of you for having the strength to say all of that to your mom. I hope you do stay. But whatever you choose will be the right thing, Grace."

Grace hugged her back. "Thanks, Ellie. I am so lucky to have a friend like you." She glanced down at her watch. "Almost time for our character class," she said, and then grinned at Ellie rather sheepishly. "It's funny, isn't it? I've only had a few counseling sessions, but I'm feeling better already about the end-of-year performances. In fact—and I can't believe I'm saying this—I'm really excited to practice our Polish dance today!"

"Yay!" Ellie cheered, jumping up. She held out a hand and pulled Grace to her feet. "Me too. Come on—let's go and get changed."

•　　•　　•　　•

The next week flew by in a flurry of exam reviews, costume fittings for the Linbury performance, and more rehearsals. A tense atmosphere had settled upon the Lower School students. Everywhere she went, Ellie noticed, there were huddles of students poring over their textbooks or practicing steps together wherever they could.

And when the exams started the following week, the tension grew thicker still. Ellie found that every morning she was waking up with the horrible feeling of unease that she always got from a bad dream. Her dreams were now dominated by lists of French verbs she couldn't get right, math equations that she couldn't solve, chemical symbols she'd forgotten . . .

Grace, however, seemed to be doing pretty well throughout it all. Ellie knew that, until recently, this extra stress would really have bothered her and shown itself in all kinds of compulsive little habits as Grace strove for control. But right now she was managing to keep everything in perspective. She had stopped practicing alone in the studio all hours of the day, and seemed to be able to get to class without constantly checking her dance kit and redoing her hair. She even went home to her mom's over the weekend and made a little joke to Ellie about how she was going to pack her bag just the once this time.

Ellie's way of managing the pressure was to get her head down every evening, work through two hours of revision, and then go and play Ping-Pong for half an hour with anybody who'd take her on.

"It's the best stress relief I can think of," she joked to her friends. "Being able to run around like crazy, after sitting all hunched over a book—plus I get to whack the Ping-Pong ball as hard as I like, and get out all that tension!"

"And you are becoming the Ping-Pong champion, too, I think," Isabelle sighed, shaking her head sorrowfully after Ellie had beaten her soundly for the third time in a week.

Ellie grinned. "That too," she said. "What a shame there isn't a Ping-Pong exam. I know I'd get an A in that, at least!"

There was a big exam schedule pinned up in the dormitory and it quickly became a ritual among the Year 7 students to take turns scribbling out each exam from the list as soon as they'd finished it. There was something enormously satisfying about obliterating the words "Science Practical 11:30" or "French Comprehension 2:30" and seeing the list gradually—*too* gradually, it seemed!—become shorter and shorter and shorter.

"I thought this week was never going to end," Sophie sighed, scribbling out the last exam—"History 2:30"—from the list. She surveyed her purple scrawls with pride. "There. They're over, girls. I hereby declare that the Year 7 exams are OVER!"

"Yippeeee!" Ellie cheered, along with her friends. She threw herself on her bed, feeling giddy with relief.

"Hallelujah, and amen," Sophie said, and then added a flourishing curtsy for good measure. She grinned at the other girls. "Now there's just the small matter of the end-of-year performances!"

Dear Diary,

The end-of-year performances have crept up on me! I've been so wrapped up in exams this week—and now it's sinking in that our Linbury performance is A WEEK FROM TODAY!

EEK!

Better dash—Matt and I are going to practice our steps together this evening. Thank goodness he's so relaxed about the whole thing; I'm hoping some of his calmness rubs off on me!

Still no further thoughts from Grace—or rather, I'm sure she's THINKING about what to do, but she's keeping it to herself. And there's no way I'm going to start badgering her about it and adding to her stress. I guess I just have to sit it out and wait for her to decide what she wants to do.

"I can't decide if I feel more excited or terrified," Ellie confided in her friends the night before their Linbury performance. They all lay in bed after lights-out—wide-awake. "Some nights I lie here thinking about how I just can't wait to dance onstage again and how amazing it's going to be, and other nights I lie here unable to stop myself from thinking about all the awful things that could happen in front of the audience—like I fall over, or trip up Matt, or . . ."

"Forget the steps, or get stage fright . . ." added Grace, with a nervous laugh.

"Get muscle cramps, or crash into somebody . . ." suggested Lara.

"Spontaneously combust with excitement," Kate said, trying to joke but sounding as anxious as the others.

"Me, I break my ankle in my dreams," complained Isabelle. "Every single night. Last night it was my arm, too!"

"Think about the applause instead," Sophie advised cheerfully. "And the bouquets of flowers that'll be chucked onstage at us all. And us all curtsying at the end, thinking, *We did it! We did it!*"

"As long as there isn't too much laughter . . . or slow hand-claps from the audience," joked Bryony.

"Or camcorders," added Grace with a shudder in her voice.

Ellie knew that Grace was thinking about her mom's plan to film her with her new camcorder.

"They're not allowed," called a voice from the other side of the dorm. It was Megan. "Sorry to eavesdrop—but you can stop worrying about that one, at least. No camcorders are permitted at any theater performances."

"Really? Phew!" Grace sighed in relief. "I'll tell my mum she has to leave hers at home, then."

"No camcorders?" said Sophie, not sounding so pleased. "My dad was going to bring his, too. I really wanted to see my performance onscreen afterward!" She gave a dramatic sigh. "Now I have to wait until I get to Hollywood!"

•   •   •   •

"Have you heard? It's a full house!" said Sophie excitedly.

Ellie nodded, her hands trembling a little as she fastened her skirt in one of the Linbury Theatre dressing rooms in the depths of The Royal Opera House.

"All those people watching us!" said Isabelle, her eyes bright.

Grace plucked fretfully at her waistband. "I hope my mum's stuck in traffic," she muttered. "Or she's lost somewhere, and is too late to be allowed into the theater. Or has been kidnapped!"

Sophie gave her arm a squeeze. "Actually, now I come to think about it, I hope my dad's lost with your mum, Grace," she said, shuddering. "He's got such a big mouth, my dad, he'll probably be standing up, shouting things out to me at the top of his voice. He's got no idea, that man." She rolled her eyes melodramatically, and the others giggled. "I can hear him now: 'Hey, Jan, there's our Soph! Will you just look at her go!'" Sophie boomed out the words in a deep, gruff voice.

"Now we know where you get it from, Soph," Lara joked.

As she giggled with the others, Ellie felt a bittersweet pang, too. Sophie was made to be a performer, she thought. It was just a shame that her performing arts school was in Manchester, so far from The Royal Ballet School.

"So . . . we all look gorgeous," Bryony said, leaning forward to tuck in a loose tendril of Sophie's hair that had worked its way loose. "Are we all feeling like prima ballerinas?"

"No!" Grace wailed at once.

"Well, I'm feeling like you're a prima ballerina," Ellie told her. "And—"

"Girls? You're next," Ms. O'Connor said, coming into their dressing room. "The boys are already backstage waiting for you. This is it!"

Ellie felt her heart skip a beat, and she grinned at her friends as a rush of adrenaline hit her. Lara and Isabelle both drew up their shoulders, as if preparing for battle. Sophie was beaming with excitement, and Kate did a last few quick stretches. And Grace . . . Grace couldn't stop fidgeting. "I can't believe this is happening," she gulped to Ellie as they left the dressing room and went to wait in the wings. "Oh my gosh—we're actually going to do this, aren't we? Get onstage in front of all those people . . . oh no, I think I'm going to be sick!"

"No, you're not," Ellie whispered back. She grabbed Grace's hand and squeezed it. "It'll all be over before we know it." She could see the boys ahead, picked out Matt in the crowd, and gave him a wave. "Let your body take over, Grace," she said quickly. "Switch your mind off, if it helps. Your legs and arms know what to do. They can do it all perfectly. The adrenaline will get you through it. I promise."

Grace was nodding, her eyes looking glassy. "Oh, Ellie," she said. "I just want to run out of the theater. I don't know if I can do it. What if—?"

"You'll be great," Ellie interrupted her gently. "Just get through it. Remember what Sophie said: Think about the applause." And then, because Ms. O'Connor was gesturing for them to partner up and get ready to go onstage, she added quickly, "Okay?"

Grace nodded. She still had her rabbit-trapped-in-headlights expression, but she was holding her head up, squaring her shoulders, taking deep breaths. "Okay," she said. "I'm thinking about the applause."

Ellie ran over to Matt, who seemed as calm as usual. "Here we go," he muttered. And, hand in hand, they walked out onto the stage with the others to take up their positions. Ellie had been so busy thinking about Grace that she'd hardly had a second to consider her own feelings about dancing in the show tonight. When she walked onto the stage, though, she was hit by the sight of a whole sea of faces in the audience and the dazzle of the stage lighting, and she felt as if the breath had been knocked out of her. *Okay, okay, don't freak out, you've done this before*, she reminded herself, as she and Matt found their starting point and stood opposite each other in anticipation, holding on to each other around the waist.

Matt smiled at her, and she smiled back, feeling her nerves

dissolve a little. It was wonderful to be here, onstage in the Linbury Theatre, partnered with her old friend, Matt. She was so glad they were in this together!

The jaunty Polish music that their piece was set to began—and Ellie's nerves suddenly stopped. Her mind became totally focused on the dance. *Sophisticated and elegant*, Ellie reminded herself as she and Matt glided through the movements, turning in a circle together, stopping for the *cabriole* step, where they clicked their heels. *Controlled, easy movements*, Ms. O'Connor said in Ellie's head. *Eyes up! Roll that arm!*

Ellie didn't dare turn to see what Grace was doing. She knew that Grace was farther upstage from her and Matt, but didn't want to distract herself by glancing over. *Focus, Ellie, focus on your own dancing*, she told herself sternly, as she and Matt let go of each other and began traveling apart for the second part of the dance. *Well, nobody's run off stage crying yet*, she told herself a second later. *I know that much—so Grace can't be doing too badly!*

Before she knew it, the music was in its last few bars. And then they were in their final positions, Matt slightly behind Ellie, with both of their left arms up and open, left knees bent, right legs low and stretched out to the side. She could hear Matt's breathing close to her ear. She could feel her own heart thumping.

And then came the applause—and it felt simply incredible!

Their eyes were all supposed to be lowered, but Ellie couldn't resist flicking hers across to see the flurry of hands clapping in the audience, the smiling faces, all turned toward the stage. Toward her, and her friends. She felt goose bumps prickle up all over her with happiness, relishing the moment as hundreds of people—including her mom and Steve, somewhere out there—all put their hands together in appreciation for the Year 7s' dancing. *We did it! We did it! And nothing went wrong!* she thought jubilantly, unable to stop the beam spreading over her face.

"Sophie Crawford, you are going to be a star!" a deep voice bellowed out from the audience and Ellie saw a man—Sophie's dad, of course!—jump up from his seat, clapping his hands above his head, while Sophie's mom tried to pull him down again. It was all she could do to stop herself from giggling out loud. He sounded exactly like Sophie's impersonation of him, too! Ellie could just imagine Sophie rolling her eyes with embarrassment.

Then the girls came together to curtsy, while the boys bowed, and the audience clapped even harder. And then—too soon, it seemed to Ellie!—they were walking off the stage again and backstage.

Matt slung his arm around Ellie's shoulders. "Well done, partner," he said, hugging her. "Not a step wrong—as usual!"

"I could say the same about you." She grinned, hugging him back.

"My DAD!" Sophie was groaning. "I take it you all heard Mr. Embarrassing Crawford out there? I'm so mortified!"

They all started giggling until Ms. O'Connor came along to shush them and herd them back to their dressing rooms. "You were all very good," she beamed. "Very good, indeed. Great job, all of you!"

Ellie disentangled herself from Matt and looked for Grace. There she was at the back of the crowd, looking bright-eyed and pink in the cheeks. "You did it," Ellie told her warmly, going over to her and giving her shoulders a squeeze. "How did it feel?"

Grace was smiling. "Nerve-racking as anything," she admitted, "but you were right about the applause. WOW. Wasn't it wonderful? I got a shiver right down to my toes!"

"I know," Ellie said, smiling at the memory. "Me too."

"And once the music started, I couldn't believe how okay I felt," Grace went on. "I did just what you said—let my body take over. That really helped. You were right. My legs knew exactly what to do. They just did it!"

Ellie laughed at the surprised look on Grace's face. "Great job, you," she said. "So the *Grand Défilé*'s going to be a breeze next week for you, won't it?" Grace's face sobered at the thought and Ellie instantly regretted saying it.

"Well . . . dancing on the smaller Linbury stage is one thing . . ." Grace said quietly, "but the main stage of The Royal Opera House? I don't know if I'll ever be ready for that."

•   •   •   •

After the rest of the performance was over, Ellie and the other

Year 7s were chaperoned to the stage door, where their parents could collect them.

Ellie couldn't stop smiling, partly with the relief that she could sleep easily at night again without dancing the steps through her head endlessly—but also because it had been so wonderful to be onstage, dancing with Matt and all her year, knowing that her mom and Steve were watching her. *Yes,* thought Ellie as she spotted her mom's smiling face outside the stage door and ran over to her, *it is just the best thing on earth, dancing in front of an audience!*

"Oh, honey!" her mom cried, hugging her tightly. "You were so good—well done!"

"Hello, Ellie," Steve said. "You looked great up there."

"You really did," Ellie's mom said, letting go and crouching a little, so that she was eye to eye with Ellie. "I am just so proud of you, you know. I could hardly believe it was my little girl up there, looking so beautiful and dancing like an angel!"

"Aww . . . Mom," Ellie said, feeling her cheeks turn pink with all the praise. "Thanks. I loved being up there. We've practiced that dance so many times, but it never felt so exciting before."

"I bet," her mom said. "Oh, and there's Grace. Grace!" she called, smiling and waving. "You were so good, sweetheart. So elegant and graceful—if you'll excuse the pun."

Grace was smiling, as was her mom. "Thank you," Grace said, bobbing a little curtsy.

"She was good, wasn't she?" Grace's mom said warmly. She put her arm around Grace. "I am so proud of you, Grace," she said quietly.

Grace's mouth went wobbly for a second, as if she was close to tears. Then she threw her arms around her mom's neck. "Thank you," Ellie heard her say in a muffled voice. "Thanks, Mum. I'm proud of me, too."

•　　　•　　　•　　　•

That evening as they were getting ready for bed, Ellie noticed with a start that Grace was humming to herself cheerfully as she put on her pajamas. Ellie smiled at the sound. She hadn't heard Grace sounding so happy for . . . well, for weeks, now that she thought about it.

"It was a good evening, wasn't it?" Ellie asked. She didn't want to put any pressure on Grace, but her subtext was clear. *Being at The Royal Ballet School is awesome, isn't it, Grace?* was what she was really trying to say.

Grace smiled and nodded. "I enjoyed it," she said, buttoning up her pajama top. She sounded faintly surprised. "Yes," she said, with certainty this time. "I really enjoyed it tonight."

Dear Diary,
My legs are aching, and I feel like I've run a marathon today—but the Linbury performance was just AWESOME. What a

buzz, hearing all those people clapping for us, and what a thrill to have danced on the Linbury stage.

I think Grace was surprised at what a good time SHE had, too. "Nothing went wrong," she kept saying in a kind of daze. "Nothing went wrong!"—like she'd been expecting the very worst to happen. She's asleep already, and it's only nine o'clock! She's smiling in her sleep, though. So, I know she had a good day.

Her mom was great, too. No pushiness. No comparisons. No "Grace, I couldn't help noticing, your arm was turning out from the wrist and not the elbow" or whatever she might have said in the past.

I'm not counting any chickens but . . . I'm secretly hoping that it's all going to change Grace's mind about staying here. Although, having said that, the pressure for the *Grand Défilé* is only going to get more intense from now on. Just a week to go! And that, of course, could change Grace's mind about The Royal Ballet School all over again. Well—here's hoping it doesn't . . .

For the run-up to the final matinee performance on the main stage at The Royal Opera House, there was a week of solid rehearsals, most of them held in The Royal Opera House rehearsal studio.

"Why am I feeling nervous about dancing in a rehearsal studio?" Grace kept fretting. "It's daft, isn't it? Just because we're in part of The Royal Opera House, I feel all flustered—and we're not even on the stage yet."

"I know what you mean," Ellie sympathized. "It is kind of weird."

"Exciting, though," Sophie said with a grin. "I can't stop looking up every time somebody walks past the studio, just in case it's a celeb." She giggled. "Do you think it would be really awful of me to take my autograph book into the dressing room with me, in case we spot anyone famous there?"

"Yes!" the others all chorused at once.

"You are just so embarrassing, Sophie," Lara chuckled. "I know you'd do it, too—go up to one of the principal dancers and ask for an autograph while they're standing there in their underwear!"

Sophie grinned again. "And your problem with that is . . . ?" she asked mock-seriously.

For all of their joking around, it was a big deal spending days in The Royal Opera House in preparation for Saturday's show. It was also really great to be able to watch the graduate students rehearse their pieces. They were soooo brilliant. It was hard for the girls to think that they could ever be that good.

After being at The Royal Ballet Lower School for almost a whole year now, Ellie was no longer awestruck when she strolled around White Lodge. She felt like she truly belonged there now. Yet it was a totally different ball game, being in The Royal Opera House building. She found herself whispering, rather than talking normally, in the corridor—and her face got flushed whenever any of the Upper School dancers were around.

On Friday, the day before the final matinee performance, the whole cast had a dress rehearsal where they went through the program accompanied by the orchestra for the first time. The first half of the program was made up of three pieces. Then came the interval, followed by a second half of two more pieces—and finally—the *Grand Défilé*. The Year 7s were only taking part in the *Grand Défilé* this year.

"But even though we don't have a huge amount to do, I still feel totally sick at the thought of being on The Royal Opera House main stage for real," Grace groaned at the end of the rehearsal. "It's huge compared with the Linbury's stage."

Ellie gave her friend a sympathetic smile. Grace had not been chosen to dance in The Royal Ballet's production last Christmas, *The Nutcracker*, as Ellie and some of the other Year 7s had. They'd already danced on The Royal Opera House main stage a number of times. At least they knew a little better what to expect.

"There will be the whole school onstage at the end, remember,

Grace," Isabelle pointed out. "So people will be looking at everybody, not just at you. It would be more scary, I think, if you were the only person on there."

"Oh, I don't know," Sophie disagreed breezily. "I'd kind of like it being alone up there."

Ellie laughed. "An evening with Ms. Crawford," she announced. "Singing, dancing, fortune-telling . . ."

Sophie winked at her. "You may laugh, Ellie Brown, but people will be paying good money for that in years to come," she said. "I'll be selling out theaters all over the country—just you wait!"

"All over the world, Soph!" Ellie replied with a grin, as she pulled on her red sweat suit over her leotard. For the *Grand Défilé*, the students would be wearing their school colors, so all of the Year 7 girls would be in their usual pink leotards and skirts. The Year 8s would be in their cornflower blue, the Year 9s in maroon, the Year 10s in royal blue, and the Year 11s in lilac.

"Hey," Lara exclaimed suddenly. "I've just realized. This time tomorrow, the matinee performance will be starting!"

"And afterward, we'll sleep for a hundred years," Grace said thankfully. "I can't wait!"

Dear Diary,
    I sooo enjoyed the dress rehearsal today.
We got to see what the graduates will be
doing for the performance—and practiced the

Grand Défilé together with everybody else in the school. It sent a shiver down my spine just rehearsing it. Goodness only knows how amazing it'll feel tomorrow, when it's for real!

The graduates were something else—they all seemed so talented and brilliant. The more I see, the more it is my number-one dream to get into Upper School when I'm sixteen, just like them.

I can hardly wait for tomorrow—just hours to go now before the big event!

"Ladies and gentlemen, would you take your seats, please? This afternoon's performance by The Royal Ballet School students will begin in three minutes."

Ellie and her friends were clustered together in the large room at the side of the main stage that was used by the Lower School students as a dressing room.

"Oh, I sooo wish we could watch it!" Sophie said longingly.

"Listen—is that the music to the first piece starting up?" Lara asked.

Everybody listened. The opening piece—a classical one—was being performed by some of the graduates.

"It's started, then," Grace whispered tensely. "Oh, I feel sick!"

Ellie grabbed one of Grace's hands, which was icy cold with nerves. "You'll be just *fine*, Grace," she told her quietly.

Toward the end of the second piece there was a flurry of excitement as some of the older girls, who were performing in the third piece, left to go and wait in the wings, ready to go onstage.

And later, two of the graduates popped by. They were still in their costumes from the classical piece they'd just performed— and looked just amazing. Ellie remembered they were named Tania Moore and Zoe Peters.

"Hi, guys," said Tania, smiling at them all. "We just wanted to say good luck. The audience seems to be loving the show— everyone's having a great time out there."

"And so will you," Zoe added. "You all look lovely, by the way."

"Th-th-thank you," Sophie managed to gulp. Everybody else just smiled, too in awe to say anything.

"Better dash—we need to get changed for the *Grand Défilé*," Tania said.

There was a stunned silence as the two graduates hurried out again.

"Wow . . ." Lara breathed, grinning. "Please God, that'll be me in . . ." she counted on her fingers, " . . . seven years time!"

Thrilled, Ellie turned to Grace. "Weren't they lovely?" she asked, but she felt the smile vanish from her face as she realized Grace had started to redo her hair.

Ellie felt a pang of alarm. Her friend was clearly feeling under pressure now. She had to try to calm Grace's nerves. "Come on, Grace," she said in a low voice, gently taking the brush from Grace's hand. "Let me help with your hair."

Grace nodded, and Ellie began brushing in long, smooth strokes. "Your fears are not going to beat you today, Grace," Ellie went on calmly. "We won't let them win. You can do this. It's going to be fine."

"I don't *want* to do it," Grace blurted out. "I don't want to go on that stage, Ellie."

Ellie wasn't going to let Grace do this to herself. "Remember how great you felt after the Linbury performance?" she reminded her lightly. "Well, I bet today going onstage is going to feel even better." She continued brushing. "And besides, even if having to go onstage today feels stressful, remember it's the very last stressful thing you have to do this whole school year, Grace. The very last one . . . And then that's it. Time out. Vacation up ahead. Six weeks of R 'n' R."

Grace breathed deeply. "Yes," she said. "That's a good way to look at it."

"It's nothing, is it?" Ellie pressed on, skillfully coiling Grace's hair into a neat, tight bun. "Three little minutes. A mere blink in your lifetime."

"A mere blink . . ." Grace mused, staring at herself in the mirror. She took another deep breath and then turned to Ellie with a faint smile. "I can do it."

"You can," Ellie agreed. "You so can, Grace."

As the music to the next-to-last piece began, Ms. Wells led them over to the wings of the stage, in readiness for the start of the *Grand Défilé*.

Grace clutched at her chest in alarm, but Ellie pretended not to notice. "There," she said, spraying Grace's hair with firm-hold spray. "Let's go—we might be able to peek out at the graduates onstage if we're lucky."

Ellie, Grace, and the rest of the girls joined up with the Year 7 boys and they waited in the wings, girls on one side, boys on the other, as quietly as they could. The music from the orchestra was swelling into a crescendo and, as Ellie and Grace craned their necks to see what was happening onstage, they saw the closing minute of the graduates' final dance.

"Awesome," Ellie whispered, her eyes glued to the scene. Their bodies were so fluid and elegant; they moved as if their bones were liquid, almost flowing across the stage.

"Just breathtaking," Grace agreed, as they watched a perfect *arabesque*.

The music faded and died, and then there was a moment's complete silence before the applause began. Ellie felt the hairs at the back of her neck prickle at the sound, and watched the flushed, pleased faces of the graduate students as they bowed and curtsied to the audience.

And then, the graduates ran offstage and the *Grand Défilé* music began.

"Good luck!" Ms. Wells whispered to them all. "And enjoy yourselves out there!"

Ellie just had time to squeeze Grace's hand before Bryony, Kate, and Alice were lining up in front of her ready to go on, and she had to take her place in the line. *This is it!* she thought. Ellie felt the most amazing exhilaration as, one by one, she and her friends ran onstage.

She and Matt performed their *balancés* and then stood in the *dégagé* pose until all of the Year 7 students were onstage. Then, along with Lara and Justin, they made up their square formation in the center and danced through the short routine that Ms. Wells and Mr. Shah had choreographed. Ellie caught Lara's eye and they smiled at each other—and then before she knew it, their routine was over, and they were running off the stage again, taking care to stand well back in order to let the Year 8 students run on and dance their piece.

"Okay?" Ellie whispered to Grace.

Grace smiled and nodded, looking quite emotional.

As each year group took its turn onstage, the excitement grew, along with the power of the music—which became more and more dramatic. Now the Year 10s were jumping and pirouetting out there.

"It is all worth it, isn't it, Ellie? To be a part of something as wonderful as this?" Grace whispered suddenly.

"Yes, Grace," Ellie replied softly. "I think so."

"I think so, too," Grace said.

Ellie felt a lump in her throat. "Grace . . . do you mean . . . ?"

They watched the Year 10s hand over to the Year 11s and Grace smiled. "Yes," she answered simply. "I've made up my mind. I want to stay."

Ellie couldn't speak. She just grasped Grace's hand and together they watched as the Year 11s made way for the first of the Upper School year groups.

The two Upper Years were amazing—and then finally, the graduates went on to perform the most spectacular *pas de deux* lifts, soaring leaps, and multiple *pirouettes*. Though the *Grand Défilé* was not yet over, the audience was already applauding, moved by the sheer brilliance of what they were seeing.

As the graduates finished their piece, Ms. Bell gave all the other students their cue.

"Here we go, Grace!" Ellie whispered.

Grace looked at her and smiled. And then, along with the others, they rushed forward.

Every year group in The Royal Ballet School streamed onstage to line up alongside the graduates.

As Ellie took her position among the two hundred or so other Royal Ballet School students, she felt such a rush of joy. She found that she had tears in her eyes. *I want to remember this moment for the rest of my life*, she thought. Standing there on The Royal Opera House main stage with her, at the end of a quite amazing first year at The Royal Ballet School, were the best friends she could ever wish for. And hundreds of pairs of hands were applauding—applauding *them*!

Too soon, it seemed, the heavy gold-braided red curtains closed. All of the students let out an enormous cheer and fell out of their lines. It was over.

Ellie turned around and saw that Sophie had immediately begun giving everyone bear hugs. She smiled. Boy, she was going to miss Sophie. But how great it had been to have her with them this special first year.

And now, coming toward Ellie, face wreathed in smiles, was Grace. Ellie's heart swelled with happiness. *The best thing about all of this,* Ellie thought as she threw her arms around Grace, *is that it goes on and on. Life at The Royal Ballet School has really only just begun.*

Year 8, here we come!

GLOSSARY

ROYAL BALLET METHOD: An eight-year system of training and methodology developed and utilized by The Royal Ballet School to produce dancers with clean, pure classical technique

ADAGE: From the musical direction *adagio*, meaning slow; slow work with emphasis on sustained positions and on balance

ALLÉGRO, GRAND ALLÉGRO, PETIT ALLÉGRO: Jumps that can be performed at various speeds

ARABESQUE: One leg is extended to the back (the name is taken from the flourished, curved line used in Arabic motifs)

ATTITUDE: *Grande pose*; one leg in the air with the knee bent either to the front or back

BALANCÉ: To rock; a swinging three-step movement transferring weight from one foot to the other

BALLONNÉ: Jumping step during which the dancer stretches one leg to the front or back, landing on the other leg with the stretched leg returning to *coup-de-pied* on closing

BARRE: The horizontal wooden bar fastened to the walls of the ballet classroom or rehearsal hall that the dancer holds for support

BATTEMENT: To beat; a beating of the legs; see *grand battement, petit battement,* and *battement frappé* for variations

BATTEMENT FONDU: To melt; a movement on one leg, bending and extending both legs at the same time

BATTEMENT FRAPPÉ: To strike; a striking action of the working foot

BOURRÉE: A series of running steps that can be done on *demi-pointe* but more frequently on full *pointe*

BRAS BAS: The rounding of the arms held in front of the thighs with a small space between the hands

CHASSÉ (also PAS CHASSÉ): A gliding step when the leg slides out and the other leg is drawn along the floor to it

COUP DE PIED: Around the "neck" of the foot; one pointed foot is placed at the calf—just above the ankle—of the opposite leg

CROISÉ: To cross; a diagonal position with one leg crossed in front of the other

DEMI-PLIÉ: A small bend (of the knees) in alignment over the toes, without causing the heel, or heels, of the foot to lift off the floor

DEMI-POINTE: Rising *en pointe* only halfway, onto the ball of the foot, not completely onto the toes

DEVELOPPÉ: The unfolding of the working leg; the leg is drawn to the knee and then extended from there

ECHAPPÉ: To escape (a movement that begins in 5th position and moves quickly to 2nd position either by sliding to the ball of the foot or as a jump from 5th position to 2nd position)

EN CROIX: In the form of a cross; a four-step movement that begins from a closed position and takes the leg to the front, side, back, and side again

FONDU: To melt (bending and extending of the legs at the same time with one leg supporting the body)

FOUETTÉ: To whip; a quick movement on one leg that requires the dancer to change direction and can be performed in a variety of ways

GLISSADE: To glide; a connecting step that begins and ends in *plié*

GRAND BATTEMENT: A throwing action of the fully extended leg in any direction with controlled lowering

GRAND JETÉ: A throwing action; a high jump from one foot to the other

GRAND PLIÉ: A deeper bend (of the knees) bringing the heels of the feet off the floor

JETÉ: A jump from one foot to the other

PAS DE BOURRÉE: A linking movement done as a series of three quick, small steps

PAS DE BOURREÉ PIQUÉ: *Piqué* means "to prick"; a quick step out on one leg to the half-toe or *pointe* position during *pas de bourrée*

PAS DE CHAT: Cat's step (because the movement is like a cat's leap); a jump where the legs are lifted and lowered separately, forming a diamond shape in the air

PETIT BATTEMENT: Small beat whereby a pointed foot "beats" in front and back of the calf—just above the ankle—of the opposite leg; this exercise is done with great rapidity

PETIT BATTERIE: A general term to describe a beating of the legs

PIROUETTE: Turn (used to describe a turn, whirl, or spin); "turns" are sometimes referred to as *tours*

PLIÉ: To bend (the knee or knees)

PORT DE BRAS: Carriage of the arms; specific movements of the upper torso and arms

POINTE: "Going *en pointe*" is to graduate from soft ballet shoes to the more demanding pointe shoes that have a hard box at the toe in the shape of a cone onto which the tips of the toes balance

RELEVÉ: To rise (used to describe a rise from the whole foot to *demi-pointe* or full *pointe*)

RETIRÉ: To withdraw (drawing up of the working foot to under the knee)

REVERENCE: A deep curtsy; performed at the end of class as a mark of thanks and respect

SAUTÉ: To jump off the ground with both feet

SISSONNE: A scissor-like movement where the dancer jumps from two feet to one foot, or from two feet to two feet

TEMPS LEVÉ: Raised movement; a sharp jump on one foot

TENDU: Stretched; held-out; tight (in which a leg is extended straight out to the front *devant*, back *derrière*, or side *à la seconde*, with the foot fully pointed)